SAVING LOU

Linda Loegel

Enjoy your time with Lou!

Linda Loegel

Saving Lou

ISBN-13: 978-1548534219

ISBN-10: 1548534218

Dedication

Saving Lou is dedicated to the men and women who have served and are now serving in the military to preserve our country's freedoms. It has been an honor to relive World War II through Lou Dyson's eyes and give thanks to the men, women, ships, and planes that helped win the war in the Pacific. Many did not come home; this book is especially dedicated to them.

It has been my intention to keep this book, while fiction, as historically accurate as possible. The major events of the USS *Hornet* and the USS *Enterprise* actually occurred during WWII.

Acknowledgement

I would like to thank the people who have contributed their knowledge and time when I've sought resource material or advice. Since I've never been a boy nor in the Navy, I needed all the help I could get to tell Lou's story.

A very special thanks to:

Members of the Cary Writers' Circle who persevered through each new chapter with me, week after week, providing valuable and constructive input.

Jim Lewis, Vietnam War veteran, for his considerable wealth of materials and ready knowledge on all things military.

Douglas Duke, U.S. Naval Academy graduate and retired Navy Reserve Commander/O-5 for putting up with my incessant emails on Navy procedure. His advice caused me to occasionally change the course I'd planned for the book, but made the book better and more accurate in the long run.

Ernest Gismondi, a veteran of WWII, for providing me with a first-hand account of basic training during the Second World War.

Thank you all for your contributions.

Prologue

July 12, 1923. Laura Dyson rolled over in the hospital bed. Pain knifed through her back and around her waist. *This baby can't come fast enough,* she moaned as she looked down the rows of beds and saw several women holding their babies and still others in the throes of labor like herself. Laura's labor had been going on for twelve hours and she felt helpless just lying in bed waiting for her baby to make an appearance. She pictured her three-year-old twins, Anna Lynn and Emma Lee, in their nighties, ready to be read to before going to bed. They were staying with her in-laws while Laura was in the hospital. Her heart ached to hold and kiss them. She pictured her husband Mike pacing back and forth in the waiting room, smoking one cigarette after another. A cigarette! Oh, how she wanted one! But the nurse had told her there was oxygen in the room, so the blessed relief of a few puffs would have to wait until she got home.

Another sharp pain caused her to cry out. Nurse Wicker turned at the sound, came toward the bed and lifted the sheet. Like everything in the sterile room, the nurse was all in white, her crisp cap pinned at an angle on top of her brown bun. Nurse Wicker called Doctor Thompson into the room. He performed an examination and announced, "Looks like this little one's ready to come into the world. Nurse, let's move her into the delivery room. Okay with you Mrs. Dyson?"

Laura grimaced as another pain shot through her. "Yes! Deliver this baby now!"

In the delivery room, Laura was given, Twilight Sleep, an anesthesia. She knew nothing more until she awoke the next morning and saw Nurse Wicker peering over her.

Laura blinked and looked around. The activity in the other beds brought back memories of labor the night before. "Nurse, where's my baby? Did I have a boy or a girl? Is it healthy?"

The nurse looked away and said, "I'll get Dr. Thompson for you," and quickly left the room.

The doctor entered the room looking tired, rumpled, and unshaven, as though he'd been at the hospital all night. "How are you this morning, Mrs. Dyson?" he asked, stifling a yawn.

Laura smiled. "I feel good; I got a good night's sleep, which is more than I can say for you. Were you up all night?"

Doctor Thompson took off his glasses and sat in the chair next to the bed. "Yes, I was. Your little ones demanded a lot of attention."

"Little ones? Plural?"

"Yes, ma'am, you have twin boys. Boy One was born at 10:12 and Boy Two was born at 10:28."

"Twins again! I can't believe it."

"Yes, twins. They're awfully small, though and we're doing our best for them. Boy One is the smallest and we have him in a bassinette in an oxygen tent with warm towels tucked in around him. I recommend you wait to name them for now."

2

"Oxygen? You mean he may not—"

"You get some sleep, ma'am, we're doing our best."

"Where's my husband?"

"He's out in the hall. He's been watching the babies through the glass since they were put into the nursery. I'll tell him you're ready to see him."

Laura ran her fingers through her hair and tried to sit up, but hadn't the strength to do so. She pasted a smile on her face for Mike's benefit.

He walked hesitantly up to her bed. "Hi, Mommy, how're you feeling?"

Laura's smile faded. "I'm fine, but the babies-- how are they?"

"They're adorable."

"But—"

"But, they're saying they're too small and might not make it, especially Boy One."

"What do you think, Mike?"

"I think our faith will get us through this one way or another. I also think we should give them names, regardless of what the doctor says. I can't just call them Boy One and Boy Two, they're real little boys who wriggle and sleep and cry and—"

"You're right, Mike, they need names. Let's name one Louis after my dad, Robert Louis Gray."

"That sounds good, and we can name the other one Lawrence after my dad, Stuart Lawrence."

"Louis and Lawrence. I love it. Which one is which?"

"Well, alphabetically Lawrence comes before Louis, so Boy One can be Lawrence and Boy Two can be Louis. Are you okay with that?"

"Yes I am. And let's make them Lawrence Stuart Dyson and Louis Robert Dyson. I think our dads will like that."

"I agree. Looks like they're bringing Louis in for you to see and hold."

Laura saw a nurse approaching carrying a squirming blanket. She eagerly held out her arms. The baby was soft; his face was contorted in an attempt to cry that came out more like a squeal. Laura counted his fingers and toes and happily confirmed he had ten of each.

Mike leaned over and kissed Laura and the baby and said, "I've been here since yesterday; I think I'd better go home and change my clothes and get a little sleep. I'll go to Mom's and look in on the girls and be back later hon."

Laura waved at Mike and looked back at Louis, so perfect and so tiny. She couldn't imagine Larry being even smaller. "Nurse," she asked, "will I be able to hold Larry?"

"Larry?"

"The one you call Boy One."

"No, I'm afraid you can't. He's very fragile and needs to be kept on oxygen. I wish you hadn't named him, it will make it harder . . . later."

The nurse took Louis back and Laura's mixed emotions spilled onto her pillow.

On the third day, Laura was strong enough to sit up. Louis was brought in to her every few hours to be nursed. She loved those moments, but she also wanted to hold and nurse Larry. In fact, she'd caused such a commotion in the ward that morning that Nurse Wicker had helped her into a wheelchair and brought her to the nursery window. A nurse in the room pushed Larry's bassinette to the window and held him up inside the tent for Laura to see. Her arms ached to hold the tiny baby and caress his little face. Too soon she was taken back to the ward and helped into bed.

She awoke after a fretful nap and saw Doctor Thompson looking down at her. She took his knitted brow and firmly set jaw as a bad sign. She looked away. "It's Larry, isn't it?"

The doctor tried to keep his voice calm and gentle. "I'm afraid so, Mrs. Dyson. He was too small to make it and died of heart failure at 4:25 this afternoon. We'll take care of the arrangements. You rest." The doctor left the ward and Laura cried for the baby she never got to hold or even touch.

Two weeks later, Mike drove Laura home while she cradled Lou close to her chest vowing to never let anything happen to this baby.

Anna and Emma were ecstatic at the sight of their new brother. Perhaps when they were old enough, Laura would tell them about their other brother, Larry.

Part One

Chapter One

August 1934. The Connecticut sun beat down on the Dyson house on Fuller Street. Laura Dyson wiped the trickle of August sweat from her forehead, dried her hands on her apron, and cautiously entered the room set aside as a home office where her husband Mike labored over his car dealership's Profit and Loss Statement. He looked up and smiled when he heard her footsteps. "Well hello, I didn't hear you come in. What. . . oh crap, what's he done now?"

"You would think that there's nothing more he could do to upset us, but somehow he keeps finding new ways." Laura said, twisting her apron as she spoke.

"Go ahead and tell me. I can't fix it until I know what *it* is."

"Remember the 1934 Cadillac you sold Dan Creary? Lou's gone and poured sand into that brand-new car. You know, the place where you put the gas. Dan says if it happens again," Laura sniffed, "he'll call the police. The boy's eleven years old, he should know better. I swear, I don't know where we went wrong with him."

Mike stood and put his hands on his wife's shoulders. "If the problem was with us, the two girls would be hellions, too. They seem to be law-abiding so we must be doing something right at least two-thirds of the time. Where is he?"

Laura pointed to the ceiling. "He's in his room where he's to stay for the rest of the night. I'm not sure if I should make him go without supper . . .." Her words fell on deaf ears as Mike was halfway up the stairs, removing his belt as he went.

Laura heard a door slam, then a shuffling sound, then the howl of her son. She hated this, but knew it was the right thing to do. Louis couldn't go on causing damage to other people's property and not pay the consequences. Still, she flinched as much at the second howl as she had at the first.

Michael Dyson, red-faced and sliding his belt back through the loops, came back into the office. "He'll be lying on his stomach for a while, I expect. I'd better go over and see Dan and see what we can do. He knows I stand by what I sell, even though this isn't the car's fault."

"Did you find out why Louis did it?"

"I'd like to know why that boy does half the stuff he does. He sure didn't get his tendencies from me," Mike gave his wife a tender pat on her rear end, "so he must've gotten them from you. Do you have a mischief gene in you somewhere? Maybe hiding behind those cute dimpled cheeks of yours?"

"Yeah, that's me, the one who never skipped class or played hooky or even took a shortcut by walking on someone's lawn. I was the original goody two shoes."

Mike winked. "You weren't so good when we were dating, in fact you were downright sinful, telling your folks you were at what's-her-name's house when you were actually with me."

Laura giggled. "Her name was Gracie and she was my best friend, so she wouldn't tell on me. Now you go take care of Dan. He won't be so nice if, heaven forbid, there's a next time."

School in New Haven started September 4th, a hot humid Wednesday, so hot even the flies couldn't find the energy to lift their wings. Louis walked slowly to the school bus that would take him to his elementary school. He was starting sixth grade where he'd be an upper classman. Next year he'd be going to the junior high school and once again he'd be relegated to low man on the totem pole, but for now, he was going to enjoy being on top. He quickened his pace, anxious to get to school where he could lord his status over the younger kids.

At recess, he and his friend Bill Landers talked about their summer activities in preparation for the What I Did During My Summer Vacation essay they knew was coming. Bill said, "I dunno what I'm gonna write about, we didn't go nowhere or do nothing. Mostly I swam and fished in the Sound. Got poison ivy; ya think that's newsworthy?"

"Nah," said Louis, "everybody gets poison ivy in the summer. Unless they stay inside for two months and don't do anything."

"What'd you do this summer?" asked Bill.

"Me, I got in trouble 'bout every other week. I spent more time in the corner than I did out of it."

"What kind of trouble?"

"Oh, you know, I broke two windows with a baseball, put dirt in Mr. Creary's new car, hid a frog in my sister's bed, set off firecrackers on July Fourth and burned my thumb, fun stuff like that."

"Wow, my dad would kill me if I did any one of those things!"

Louis grinned. "As you can plainly see, I'm still here, alive and well. Let's go tell that third grader she has to eat a handful of dirt if she wants to be our friend."

"Nah, I'm not like you. I don't wanna get in trouble."

"You're no fun. No wonder you had a boring summer."

Chapter Two

October 1934. Lou sat on his bed and looked around his room. He had everything a young boy could ever want—airplane models hanging from his ceiling, an Erector set, Lionel electric train tracks that ran around his room and over a small bridge, a set of Lincoln Logs, Tinker toys, and a pair of clamp-on roller skates. His parents told him he wasn't to play with any of his toys for the rest of the day; instead, he was to think about what he'd done and write an apology.

He opened his notebook, took out a fresh sheet of lined paper, and began writing. *Dear Mom and Dad. I'm sorry I messed up; I won't do it again. Love, Lou.* Okay, he thought, that was easy. He took the piece of paper downstairs and proudly handed it to his mother. "Here," he said, a look of satisfaction on his face.

Laura read the so-called apology and handed the note back to Lou. "Louis, this is just a generic apology, it could be for anything. I want to know that you know what you did wrong and why you'll never do such a thing again. Go back upstairs and this time write a real apology. Go on now."

Lou pouted and slowly walked back up to his room. Sitting cross-legged on his bed, he fumed to himself, *Why do I do these stupid things? Why did I think it was funny to put salt in the sugar bowl? I should have known it would ruin Mom's coffee and then she'd yell at me. Annie and Em never did dumb stuff like that when they were my age. What's wrong with me? Do I have screw-up blood in me?*

Lou pulled out a fresh sheet of paper, held it close to his face and began to write. *Dear Mom and Dad, I'm real sorry I put salt in the sugar bowl. Anna and Emma would never do that. And if Larry had lived instead of me, he probably wouldn't have done it, either. I'm sure you wish my brother was the one who survived and not me. He wouldn't do the stupid things I do and you'd all be happier with him than you are with me. I hope you'll forgive me. Louis.*

Lou crept down the stairs, left the note on the phone table, and silently walked out the door.

Laura finished putting supper on the table and called upstairs for Lou to come down and eat. When the family was gathered at the table, she noticed her son wasn't with the others. She went to the staircase and called again, but got no answer. Walking back to the dining room, she noticed a folded piece of paper by the phone, picked it up, read it and immediately handed Mike the note. Worry lines framed his face. He called upstairs, but got no response. Mike and Laura looked at each other and realized their son was missing. They rushed outside and ran down the street calling Lou's name.

Lou sat on a bench in front of his father's car lot wishing he'd thought to bring a jacket. The October air had turned cold. He wasn't sure where he'd go or where he'd spend the night, but he knew he couldn't stay in the home where he caused so much trouble.

"You go that way," said Mike, "and I'll go down this street. He couldn't have gotten too far. You said you talked to him about an hour ago, right?"

"Right. I should never have complained about his apology note."

"You did the right thing, now we just have to find him."

Mike started down the street toward Dyson's Cadillacs and there, huddled on a bench against the wind, was his son. "Louis! Am I glad I found you! Come on, let's get you home and out of the cold."

On their way, Mike caught up with Laura and the three of them walked back into the house. Anna and Emma were reading the letter, but stopped when their parents entered with Lou.

"Let's get some hot food into you, son," said Mike, "then we can sit and talk about your letter. Okay?"

Lou hung his head. "Okay."

After a subdued meal, Laura sent the fourteen-year-old twins to their room so she and Mike could sit and talk alone with Lou.

Laura cleared her throat. "I don't know where you got the idea that you weren't wanted around here, sweetheart, but I'm here to tell you that's not true. I spent twelve hours in labor, back in 1923, just so you and your brother could be brought into this world. Right, Mike?"

"Yeah, I about wore a hole in the waiting room carpet, pacing back and forth." He looked at Lou. "When I finally got to see you, I thought you were both just about the handsomest baby boys I'd ever seen."

"Really?"

"Really. And I'm sorry that Larry didn't make it; his heart just wasn't strong enough for him to survive. But you did; in fact, you fought real hard to live and to grow up."

"So why am I so different? The girls don't get into trouble like I do."

Mike squeezed Lou's hand. "For one thing, girls are naturally different. They don't seem to have the penchant for getting into trouble that us boys do." Mike looked straight at Lou. "However, just being a boy doesn't excuse all the, as you said, stupid things you do. You need to stop thinking Larry would have been a better child. There's no way of knowing what he would have been like, but I'm here for you if you ever want to talk and work this out together. Got it?"

"Got it. Thanks, Dad. Mom, can I do the dishes for you tonight?"

Laura was shocked at her son's offer. Moments later, she rose and whipped off her apron and tossed it to Lou. He tied the frilly thing around his waist, the hem reaching way below his knees. Watching the iridescent soap bubbles float into the air, then pop, reminded him of a recurring dream in which he was just about to grab something he wanted when it flew out of his grasp and disappeared. In the morning, he was never able to remember what he was reaching for, just that something was always beyond his reach. He stood at the sink and opened his hand, letting a bubble land gently on his palm. He closed his hand to keep the bubble, but as soon as he did, the pretty sphere was gone, leaving a wet spot on his hand. He sighed, wiped a tear from his cheek with a soapy hand, and attacked the dirty dishes.

Chapter Three

March 1935. Laura walked into Lou's room on a Saturday afternoon and found him reading *Tom Sawyer* by holding the book close to his face. Laura laughed, "Looks like you've got your nose in a good book!"

Lou chuckled at his mother's joke and continued reading. Laura pulled the book down to a proper reading position, but as soon as she left the room, Lou brought the book to his face again.

Lou came home from school, reached in his pocket and pulled out a note from his teacher. Laura took the note, thinking *This can't be good.* She unfolded the wrinkled paper and began to read:

Mr. and Mrs. Dyson, it pains me to have to tell you that Louis's work is not up to par with the other students. He fails nearly every spelling test and is close to failing arithmetic. Since it is March, he still has time to bring his grades up before the end of the year and be promoted to seventh grade.

Laura glanced up at the kitchen clock as though it would confirm what month they were in. She sighed and continued reading.

It has been my observation that Louis has trouble seeing the blackboard from where he sits in class. I've tried moving him closer to the front, but he returns to his usual seat as soon as I turn my back. Extra homework and making him write I will do better one hundred times, haven't worked. It is my feeling that his problem seeing may explain his disruptive behavior. I would suggest you get his eyes examined to see if he needs glasses.

Laura read the last line over and over. Maybe that was why Lou always held papers so close to his face. If all it took was glasses to get his grades back up . . . just the thought of a new and improved Lou was enough to get her heart racing. She ran down the street to the showroom to tell Mike. She found him sitting in a new Cadillac, running his hands over the smooth steering wheel and staring off into space.

Laura walked over and tapped him on the shoulder. Mike slowly turned to look at her, then resumed staring at nothing.

"Mike, are you okay?"

"Yeah. I suppose. Not really."

"What's the matter? What's going on?"

Mike looked down, ran his hand over the dashboard, and started to say something but the words caught in his throat. Laura waited patiently.

After a while, Mike got out of the car, gently closed the door, and went into his office. Laura followed him. He pushed aside a stack of papers and settled down on the corner of his desk. Laura sat in a chair, holding the note from school. Mike picked a letter off the desk and wordlessly waved it in the air.

What's that?" asked Laura.

"You go first," said Mike. "What do you have?"

17

Laura read the note. When she got to the last line about Lou needing an eye exam and probably glasses, she was smiling, but her smile quickly faded when she looked up and saw the worried look on Mike's face. "I thought you'd be as happy as I am to hear there may be a reason why Lou misbehaves as much as he does."

"I am."

"Well, if you don't mind my saying so, if that's you being happy, I wouldn't like to see you when you're upset. What's going on?"

Mike cleared his throat. Coughed. Cleared his throat again and spoke low. "It would appear that this Depression is now affecting us, too. I thought because we sold Cadillacs to well-off customers, we could distance ourselves from what so many other people are going through these days."

"But . . .."

"But, it seems our well-off customers are starting to feel the pinch, too. A new, expensive car is the last thing they're looking to buy. Food and clothes come first, as well they should." Mike held out the letter he was holding. "This letter is from the bank. They want us to pay our loan on each of these cars now. Not wait until they're sold."

"Oh, Mike! How can we do that? It would cost a small fortune."

"I know. It's going to take every cent we have. Let's just say it's bad timing for Lou to need an eye exam and glasses, as much as I want him to have them."

"It's 1935; how much longer can this Depression last?"

Chapter Four

Mike Dyson lowered the price of his cars on the assumption that anything he got from selling them was better than having to pay the loans off while the cars were unsold. His profit wasn't as much as he'd hoped, but at least he *had* a profit. For the cars that didn't sell even with the reduced price, he and Laura scraped together every penny they had in order to comply with the bank's letter and pay off the debt on their inventory.

To make ends meet, Laura and Mike started selling their personal items. The day Laura's grandmother's opal ring was sold at a fraction of its worth, Laura secluded herself in her room, soaking her apron with the tears that kept falling.

Mike fought against selling the set of golf clubs he'd bought on a trip to Scotland, but with golf courses closing up left and right, he had no use for them. On the other hand, the money the clubs brought in would enable Lou to get a pair of eyeglasses after an exam confirmed he did, indeed, have trouble seeing.

At the optometrist's office, Lou tried on every pair of glasses that weren't clearly girlie looking. He finally settled on a pair of black rimmed glasses that sat nicely on his nose. His father said, "Well now, don't you look just like Sigmund Freud."

"Who?" Lou asked.

"Don't worry about it," said Mike. "Just know he's a very smart doctor who interprets dreams."

"Dreams? Really?"

"Really."

When Lou and Mike entered their house on Fuller Street, Laura put her hands to her face and said, "Oh my! Don't you look like an intellectual."

The twins came down the stairs, took one look at Lou and burst out laughing. "Hey look, it's Four Eyes."

Lou glared at them, whipped off his glasses, and threw them to the floor. He was about to stomp on them when his father grabbed him and held him tight. "Hold on, son, it took a lot for us to get you those glasses and we expect you to take care of them. You're going to find that people will always make comments about something new and different and you'd better learn how to deal with them." Mike turned to Anna and Emma. "As for you two, I would expect you to know better. Now apologize to your brother."

"Sorry."

Lou sank onto the sofa cushions and tossed his new glasses on the coffee table. He scowled as he watched them take a hop, then stare back at him, taunting him just as his sisters had done. He heard a noise and looked up to see Anna and Emma enter the room. They plopped down, one on either side of him. He glared at them. "Whadda you two stink faces want?"

Anna, being the oldest of the twins by five minutes, twirled her brown pony tail with her fingers and spoke first. "Hey shrimp, you know we love you. We were just kidding with you."

"Right," said Emma. "We wouldn't hurt you for the world, you know that. You're our little Lou Guy." She tried to give him a hug, but he swerved to avoid getting touched by her.

Anna patted his leg. "Do you remember, Louie, when Dad was teaching us girls to waltz so we could go to the school dance? We kept walking on his feet and tripping over our own."

Lou smiled.

"Yeah, you remember. You laughed at us a lot that night. That's what siblings do. That's the best way us kids can help each other prepare for life out there." She gestured toward the front door. "You know the kids at school are gonna call you Four Eyes as soon as they see you."

"Right," said Emma, "and you'd better be prepared for it. Actually, I think those glasses make you look studious. So there."

Lou reached for his glasses and put them on, smiling first at Anna, then Emma. They tousled his hair and went up to their room.

Chapter Five

Five years earlier, October 1930. Mike Dyson sat in the living room by the fireplace in his velvet easy chair with its crocheted arm covers. His three children sat in a semi-circle on the floor in front of him. Ten-year-old Anna and Emma had asked him to tell them the story of how he and Laura had met. Lou, seven, played on the floor with a truck, only half listening to his father.

"I was born in 1898, and . . ..

"Not that far back," the girls shouted, "start with when you met Mommy."

"Oh, okay, since you don't want to hear the *good* stuff. It was a warm spring day in 1916 and I was working as a soda jerk at Watson's Drug store making sodas and banana splits and such at the counter. Now old man Watson was a character in his red suspenders and handlebar mustache, let me tell you. He taught me everything I know about being a jerk. A soda jerk, that is." Mike looked off into space.

"What about Mommy!" the girls said in unison.

"Oh yes. Well, one day this cute high school junior walked into the drug store with two of her friends and they each ordered a banana split. I made normal splits for her friends, but added a fourth scoop of ice cream and put an extra cherry on top of hers. I thought she was the cutest girl I'd ever seen."

Laura stood in the doorway, smiling as she listened and remembered.

"The next day, she came in by herself and I made her banana split even more special. She ate it without saying much, but she had this cute little habit of wiping the corner of her mouth with her pinky finger and then licking her finger. I was so busy watching her, I didn't even notice that other customers were sitting on the stools waiting to order, until old man Watson yelled at me."

"Did you get her name?"

"I sure did. I wasn't about to let her get away this time without finding out who she was and where she lived. Pretty soon this girl, Laura, and I were dating. Weren't we honey?" He looked up at Laura in the doorway. She nodded and blew him a kiss.

Lou continued to play with his truck. It was obvious this conversation was going nowhere.

Emma asked, "So when did you decide to get married?"

Mike pulled his cardigan around him. "You three are all too young to know, but there was a war going on over in Europe and a lot of talk that the United States might just get involved in it. Let me see, we met in the spring of sixteen and in April of seventeen, this country declared war on Germany. I was almost nineteen and your mom was a senior in high school by then. A month later, May it was, Congress instituted the draft so I had no choice but to join the Army. You've seen the posters of a bearded man pointing his finger at you saying, "Uncle Sam Wants You!"

The girls nodded and Lou stopped playing and paid attention to his father.

"I don't know why Uncle Sam wanted me, I was just a dumb old soda jerk, but it seems he figured he could make a man out of me and let me tell you, he did, too. In the spring of eighteen, I boarded a ship with hundreds of other guys and we were off to Europe. I hated to say goodbye to this pretty lady standing in the doorway, but my Uncle Sam wanted me."

"What did you do in the Army?" asked Anna.

Mike puffed on his cigarette and blew smoke rings toward Lou. "Seems once the Army taught me to drive, I had a knack for it, so they made me an ambulance driver. I was stationed in France with my buddy Morris, God rest his soul. We transported the sick and injured to an aid station. A lot of the guys only had the flu, but we saw our share of war injuries, too."

"Like what?" asked Lou, now fully engrossed in his father's story.

"Like bullet and shrapnel wounds and some other things I won't tell you; you don't need nightmares. I was lucky 'cause although we were caught in the crossfire now and then, other than taking a bullet in the leg while lifting a soldier into the ambulance, I escaped unscathed."

"Where? And what about Morris?" asked Lou.

Mike pointed to just below his knee, then paused. "I'm afraid Moe wasn't so lucky. When I got the soldier loaded into the ambulance, I turned around to tell Moe we'd better scram, and there he was, lying in the dirt. He'd been hit in the chest and was barely breathing. I got him into the ambulance and drove lickety-split to get help. Normally, he was the one in the back tending to the patient while I drove. This time, there was no one to tend to him." Mike looked at the floor. "He didn't make it."

"Did you get any medals, Daddy?" asked Emma.

"Yeah, I got the Purple Heart, but I'd rather there was never a war in the first place."

"So, about Mom," Anna pleaded.

"Oh yeah. Mom." Mike grinned. "The war was over in November and I came home, we got married, you twins were born and three years later," he looked at Lou, "you were born. The war was a piece of cake compared to raising you three!"

Lou went back to playing with his truck, pretending it was an ambulance and he was saving lives with bullets whizzing around him.

Chapter Six

On Lou's first day at school with his new glasses, he discovered his sisters were right; the other kids did make fun of him. The first child to call him Four Eyes was Tommy Watson. Lou glared at him and walked away. By recess, four other boys had called him Four Eyes and by then he was angry. The next boy to taunt him wasn't as lucky as the others. Lou shoved his glasses at his friend Bill, put up his fists and took a stance like the great boxer, Max Baer, daring the unlucky contestant to call him that name again. The boy, in a moment of insanity, did just that. Fists went flying in all directions and soon the boys were on the ground scuffling with each other while the whole sixth grade class formed a circle around them and watched, rooting for whomever was on top at the moment.

When the bell rang, the teacher came out and stopped the fight. Lou had a cut lip and torn shirt; his opponent's nose was bleeding and tears streaked his dirty face. They were both sent to the principal's office. Mr. Cramer, a no-nonsense man who didn't tolerate fighting, made the boys shake hands, which they did in a flash, barely touching each other. On their way back to class, they continued to push and shove in an effort to outdo one another.

When school was over, Lou walked into the house and attempted to get to his room before his mother could see him. No such luck. She grabbed him by the dirty collar and said, "What on earth happened to you? Don't tell me you were fighting."

"Okay, I won't."

"Were you fighting?"

"Yes'm."

"Why?"

"The kids called me Four Eyes. I don't wanna wear these stupid glasses anymore!"

"Can you see the blackboard better?"

"Yeah."

"Then you will continue to wear them. We'd better come up with a way for you to handle the other kids. You can't fight every one of them. Now go wash up and put some ice on that lip."

Being made fun of didn't sit well with Lou. He was used to being the one who picked on the younger kids; he wanted no part in being the one who got picked on. At least once a week, he came home with his clothes torn from a fight at recess. Before long, his glasses sported tape over the nose piece that had broken when he forgot to take the glasses off before throwing the first punch.

"That does it," said his father during supper one evening. "We need to teach you how to defend yourself."

Laura looked shocked. "You're not going to teach him how to box are you?"

Mike laughed. "No, he does enough of that already and look where it's gotten him. You know, when I was his age, the kids all called me a name I didn't like."

Mike had the rapt attention of his three children. "What was it?" Emma asked.

"If I tell you, you must never repeat it again, understand?"

They all nodded; they would have agreed to anything in order to hear what their father had been called.

Laura looked at Mike and smiled, wondering what on earth anyone could find wrong with her handsome husband.

Mike cleared his throat. "I was shorter than the other boys in my sixth-grade class. Seems they'd all started their growth spurts and I was still a runt compared to them."

Lou stared at his father. "What'd they call you?"

Mike focused on Lou. "They called me Wee Little Michael."

"Did it bother you?" Lou asked.

"Of course. Grampa Dyson always told me I might grow as tall as him, but I didn't believe it because I saw no evidence of it. I was miserable."

"What did you do, Daddy?" asked Anna.

Mike plunged his fork into the slice of apple pie sitting in front of him. "At first I did what Lou's been doing. I got mad. I tried to fight every kid who called me that name. I got beat in every fight 'cause they were all bigger than me, so that strategy clearly wasn't working. Is it working for you, Lou?"

Lou looked down at his pie. "No, sir."

"I thought not. So then I tried tattling on them which only made things worse. Now they started the fight instead of me, which still didn't end up well for me. So, I figured I had to come up with something different. Gramma Dyson helped me with this since she was tired of mending my clothes all the time. With her advice, the next time a boy called me Wee Little Michael, I didn't let it get to me. You know, if bullies have no one to bully, they lose interest."

Lou took a gulp of milk. "That's it? You just didn't let it bother you?"

Mike smiled. "Basically. But I also turned their taunts around and said, 'Great things come in small packages, you know.' They didn't know how to respond to that. From then on, they left me alone. And of course, once I started growing, no one laid a hand on me."

"So, what can I say?" asked Lou.

Laura spoke up. "You might say something like, 'Just as two heads are better than one, four eyes are better than two.' Let them know they're not getting to you. Make a joke of it and soon they'll be laughing with you instead of at you."

"I'll try," said Lou. "But it better work, 'cause I'm getting tired of being made fun of."

Anna put her arm across Lou's shoulders. "Now that you know how it feels, just make sure you don't pick on other kids."

"Oh, I wouldn't," said Lou, angelically.

Chapter Seven

Ten Years Earlier, July 1925. At a July Fourth cook-out in their back yard, Mike turned the hamburgers and hot dogs on the grill and breathed in the heady aroma of onions sizzling in a small pan next to the meat. While Laura made trips from the kitchen to the picnic table carrying potato salad, baked beans, and watermelon, her mother-in-law, Alice Dyson, brought out the paper plates, drinks, and cups. Laura's five-year-old twin girls played with a ball on the lawn and Lou, nearly two, bounced up and down in a walker, a wooden toy car in one hand and a cracker in the other.

Stuart Dyson sat in a lawn chair drinking lemonade and sputtering, "This stuff isn't fit for human consumption. This Prohibition nonsense better be over soon so's I can get a good bottle of beer again."

When the food was but a fulfilling memory and the marshmallows were roasted, Stuart took Mike aside to discuss a plan that had been forming in his mind. "Son," he said, "your mother and I have been talking and we'd like to do something for you and Laura, if you're interested."

Mike stopped scraping the grill and watched his father wipe a drop of ketchup off his shirt. "What's that, Dad?"

Stuart cleared his throat. "Your mother and I are getting on in years and are thinking about moving to Florida. So, we'd like to turn our car dealership and repair shop over to you. But, there's a catch."

"Florida? To me? Wow! When did all this happen? I don't care what the catch is, I'm interested."

"The catch is, you'd have to come work for me and start at the bottom. I want you to learn how to repair the cars, how to wash and wax them, how to sell them, how to do the paperwork, how to order inventory and such. You'd start at the bottom, like I said, learning the ropes so you'll know the business inside and out. In a few years, we'll draw up the papers and the business will be yours. Are you still interested?"

Mike collapsed onto a lawn chair and exhaled. Reaching out, he grasped his father's hand. "Wow, Dad. I'll talk to Laura, of course, but as far as I'm concerned, this is a once-in-a-lifetime opportunity. And like you said, learning from the ground up is the only way to run a business."

Mike motioned to Laura to come over and she and Alice, who had a wide grin on her face, pulled up lawn chairs next to the men. Stuart nodded at Alice as a way of saying *I told him.* Mike relayed to Laura what his father had just offered and when he finished, she jumped up and hugged Stuart, then Alice.

"I guess," said Mike, "that that's a yes."

"Yes!" said Laura. "We can never thank you enough for giving us this start. Imagine! We'll own our own business."

The next day, Mike gave his notice at Watson's Drug store where he had worked up to manager, and soon became an employee at his father's dealership and garage. For years he'd heard his father talk about the car business, but now that it was more than talk, he became a sponge soaking up everything there was to learn.

Mike's first training task was washing floors. In the garage, he had to use a soap that cleaned up dirty grease stains. In the showroom, he learned how to keep the floors sparkling and inviting. His father not only sold new cars, he also took in older cars for repair. The head mechanic, Gus Olafson, took Mike under his wing and showed him the inner workings of cars. Mike was curious to learn and in no time new words entered his vocabulary—pistons, manifold, spark plugs, fan belt, starter crank, exhaust pipe. So many parts to cars that Laura didn't even know existed. Within months, there wasn't a car brought into the shop that Mike couldn't get running again.

One night after a hard day at work, he walked into the kitchen and held out his arms to hug Laura, but she laughed and backed away when she saw his greasy hands and coveralls. Throughout supper he talked animatedly about how to fix brakes and change oil. Laura liked this new fire that burned in Mike and how each day brought them closer to owning their own business.

A few weeks later, Mike showed up at work dressed in a suit and tie. He was now ready to demonstrate to his customers the joy and pride that comes from owning a new Cadillac. On his first sale, Stuart showed him how to fill out a Bill of Sale and collect license and registration fees. After that, Stuart showed him how to order new cars as well as car parts.

Within two years of watching his son excel at all aspects of a car dealership, Stuart determined that Mike was ready to take over the business of Dyson's Cadillacs. The two couples went out to dinner to celebrate, toasting the new venture by holding up goblets filled with Nehi soda, much to Stuart's dismay. It didn't look like Prohibition was ending anytime soon after all.

Feeling comfortable leaving Mike as head of Dyson's Cadillacs, Stuart and Alice packed their bags and moved to Florida to escape the cold winters of Connecticut. They left with one request–that they have a place to stay when they come north to see their grandchildren once a year. Laura assured them there would always be a place for them in their home.

Chapter Eight

September 1935. According to the newspapers, the Depression was getting better, but relief was not at all apparent to Mike and Laura. Their car sales were still down and, reluctantly, they were forced to lay off a salesman. The only upside was that their repair shop was doing well as more and more customers opted to do whatever it took to keep their current vehicles running rather than having to buy a new car.

The second week of his seventh-grade class, Lou came home with his glasses broken beyond repair. A bully had made fun of him and before Lou could come up with a retort, fists were flying. His glasses fell off and got stepped on in the melee.

At supper, Lou kept his head down and even ate his vegetables, hoping no one would notice that his glasses were missing. As it turned out, his parents were smarter than he gave them credit for.

"Where are your glasses?" asked Mike.

"Um, I left them somewhere."

"Really? Where?"

"I don't remember."

"Think harder, then tell us the truth."

Lou put down his fork and lowered his voice. "I broke 'em at school. The glass is broken and the frames are bent. I'm sorry."

Laura shook her head and swiped at her eyes with a napkin. With debts piling up, this was not what she wanted to hear. She looked at Mike in a plea for help.

Mike scooted his chair away from the table and placed his hands firmly on his knees. Focusing on Laura, he said, "I've been contemplating something lately and I think now is the time to tell you my plan."

Four pair of eyes turned to look at Mike. "What plan?" asked Laura. "Do you want the kids to go to their rooms while we talk?"

"No. This involves the kids." Not a sound came from Anna, Emma, and Lou as they sat in rapt attention, awaiting their fate.

"Anna and I didn't do anything wrong," said Emma. "So why us?"

Mike had learned patience in the Army and could stay calm in the midst of bullets flying, so a family discussion with teenagers was a walk in the park. "I didn't say anyone did anything wrong."

"Well then . . .."

"What I'm suggesting is that since our business is called Dyson's Cadillacs, I think ALL the Dysons ought to be involved. Anna and Emma, you'll start working in the office after school and learn filing and answering the phone. Little by little, you'll know as much about the business of selling cars as I do."

The twins' eyes twinkled and they hugged each other at the thought of doing real work in a real office.

Lou spoke up. "You don't want me, do you; I'm only twelve."

Mike smiled. "On the contrary, I especially want you."

"You're not gonna put me in the office doing girl's work, are ya?"

Mike shook his head and laughed. "No, but if I wanted you to, you'd do it and do it with a smile on your face. Right, son?"

"I guess."

"No," said Mike, "what I see for you is to start in the repair shop."

"You mean I can learn how to fix cars?" Lou smiled as though he'd just been handed a huge bowl of chocolate ice cream.

"Eventually," said Mike. "but first, you'll learn the same way I did. You'll start by learning how to wash floors."

Lou frowned; his ice cream had suddenly disappeared. "Aww, really?"

"Hey, you break your glasses, you have to earn the money to buy new ones. That's the way this country works. Nobody gets something for nothing."

"Oh."

"Trust me, you're a smart kid so I don't expect it'll take you long to get the hang of it. Before you know it, you'll be learning about motors and brakes and such."

"Do you really think so, Dad? Ha ha, girls, I get to do *real* work. Man-type work."

Laura had been taking all of this in, glancing from one family member to another as they spoke. Now it was her turn. "To start your education, you three can clear the table and do the dishes while your father and I take a walk." She held out her arm to Mike and together they sauntered out the door.

When the front door had closed, she asked Mike, "And just what is it you have planned for *me*? Do you figure I don't have enough to do around here?"

Mike patted her arm. "That's just it, honey, you have plenty to do keeping us all in line; that ought to be enough of a job for anyone."

Chapter Nine

Anna and Emma entered their home economics class and took seats next to each other. They looked around the room, delighted that they were now sophomores in high school and would be taking up sewing this year. After spending last year's Home Ec class learning to make pies, cakes, and casseroles, the twins looked forward to this year where they'd get to make their own clothes.

And they wouldn't be just alike, either. Fifteen years of being dressed alike was enough; the girls wanted to explore their own individualities. Although they looked alike in the face, Emma was taller and lankier than Anna. Not by much, but enough to tell them apart. Emma's favorite color was blue, Anna preferred green. Emma Lee's hair was reddish brown; Anna Lynn's was a dark brown. This was the year they would become Emma and Anna instead of "The Twins."

The eager chatter of the students subsided when Miss Hughes walked in and closed the door. She looked elegant in a tan print dress with ruffled cap sleeves. To top off the outfit, she wore a jaunty brown hat with flowers on the side, sitting askew over her blonde hair that was wrapped up in a bun. "Good afternoon, class," she chirped, "my name is Miss Hughes and we'll be making our own clothes this year." She unpinned her hat and placed it on the desk.

Emma raised her hand. "Did you make your dress? Will we be able to make something like that?"

Miss Hughes nodded. "You girls will be amazed at what you can make this year with the right material, right pattern, and proper instruction." She took attendance and then explained the room layout. "On this side of the room, we have four large tables for laying out your material and pinning the pattern. You will do hemming and other hand sewing at your desk. Over here, we have ten old but still quite usable sewing machines. We have more girls than machines, so you will have to take turns. On this back wall, you can see we have spools of thread, material, and patterns for you to choose from."

Miss Hughes then sat at one of the sewing machines and asked the sixteen students to gather around as she explained how to thread the machine, where and what the bobbin was, and how they were to properly work the treadle with their feet. "Remember," she cautioned, "this can be a dangerous machine if you're not paying attention. More than one student has pierced her finger when she got too close to the needle while it was in operation."

Emma and Anna picked out a simple skirt pattern to start with and couldn't wait to go home and show their mother. Laura was pleased; having the girls make their own clothes would certainly help their finances as well as give the girls a good head start toward being housewives and mothers someday. Home Economics had always been Laura's favorite class and she was pleased her girls liked it as well. A woman can never go wrong learning how to cook and sew.

After school, the girls took their English and History homework over to the office of Dyson's

Cadillacs. Mike showed them how to answer the phone, not that it was ringing much lately. He then showed them how to file alphabetically and which file cabinet was for new car invoices and which was for repairs. The girls caught on quickly and were able to do their homework between calls.

When Lou got home from school, he had a snack then went to the repair shop. Mike met him at the door and introduced him to Gus. Gus was in his forties, had blond hair flying in all directions, and striped coveralls covered with grease. His face was pockmarked and he bore a scar that ran along his right cheek. Lou held out his hand, but when Gus extended a greasy palm, Lou quickly put his own hand at his side and said, "Nice to meetcha."

Mike grinned. "Lou, Gus is my number one mechanic, been here since Grampa owned the business. You'll learn a lot from him. I'll leave you two alone now. Gus, don't go easy on him!"

Lou wanted to glare at his dad, but he was too excited to be working in the shop where he'd soon know more than anybody about how to fix cars. He figured that in two or three months, he'd be the number one mechanic in New Haven. His dream bubble burst when Gus told him to pick up the bag of cornmeal standing against a wall and start his apprenticeship by sprinkling it over the puddle of oil and grease on the floor. Gus then rubbed a bit of cornmeal on his own hands and showed Lou how it absorbed the grease. Lou was then told to get a can of soap powder from a metal shelf and pour it over the cornmeal. "Now," said Gus, "pick up that deck broom and start scrubbing the floor, ya?"

Lou picked up the broom that was taller than he was and made a few swipes at the dirty area. "Put some muscle into it, son," said Gus. Lou pressed down harder and saw that his efforts paid off; the floor was indeed getting cleaner.

"Good job," said Gus. "We need ta keep this floor clean, ya? Otherwise, we end up tracking grease on the showroom floor. You do the shop floor good this week and next week we'll move up to big time, ya know, cleaning the showroom floor."

During supper that night, Laura noticed that while the girls chatted endlessly about school, her son was quieter than usual. He ate bent over his plate as though it was an effort to sit up. She mused, *Mike was right, a little hard work is good for him. He'll be too tired to get into trouble.*

Chapter Ten

Lou's second week on the job had him working in the showroom surrounded by gleaming new Cadillacs arranged invitingly on the mirror-finish floor. Gus outfitted him with a bucket of suds and a mop and exact instructions on how to wash the floor without splashing any water on the expensive cars. Gus stood off to the side and watched his protégé studiously concentrate on the task at hand, then as Lou gradually lessened his white-knuckle grip on the mop handle once he found his rhythm.

On the radio, Shirley Temple was happily singing about the Good Ship Lollipop and Lou pretended he was swabbing the ship's deck. Gus grinned. Figuring Lou had the situation under control, the ace mechanic walked back to the garage to do a lube job.

Lou started dancing between the cars with the mop as his partner. One moment they were bowing and twirling and the next moment Lou slipped on the wet floor. The mop went in one direction and Lou slid into the bucket of water, knocking it over and splashing water in every direction. The bucket crashed into one car and Lou crashed into another.

Gus ran into the room and found Lou sitting on the floor holding his head. His clothes were soaking wet and Shirley Temple was exiting the Good Ship Lollipop.

Gus examined Lou then checked out the two cars. All three would survive, though a little worse for wear. Gus ordered Lou to clean up the watery mess on the floor, then go home and change his clothes and come right back. When Lou got back to the shop, his father returned from running an errand. He saw nothing out of place until Gus motioned to him to come into the showroom.

"Boss," said Gus, "we have a slight problem. I dropped a mop bucket and left a small scratch on the side of this here car. I can have it fixed up like new, but I wanted you ta see it first."

Mike scratched his head and looked at Gus, then Lou. "You did this, Gus?"

"Ya, I did. Don't you know the water spilled over and the bucket slipped right out of my hand and afore I knew it, it had landed against the car. Don't worry, boss, I'll have it right as rain in no time. It'll give me a chance to show the boy here how to fix a scratch."

"Okay," said Mike. "But be more careful next time."

"I will."

When Mike left, Lou scrunched his eyes and gave Gus a puzzled look. "Whatcha do that for, Mr. Gus? You didn't scratch that car. I did."

"Did ya learn something from it, boy?"

"Yeah, to be more careful next time."

"Okay then, lesson learned and we won't talk about it again. Now go get me that cloth and tin can sitting by the wax. You're about to get your first lesson in body shop repair."

Lou did as he was told and in that moment, it seemed Gus had grown a foot taller.

During supper, Mike told Laura about Gus' carelessness. "Funny," he said, "he's never done anything like that before. He's always extra careful around the new cars."

Lou said not a word; instead, found great interest in the mound of mashed potatoes on his plate.

Chapter Eleven

Lou kissed his parents goodnight, quickly swiped a toothbrush across his teeth, pulled on his pajamas, and jumped into bed. He put on the new glasses he'd received as payment for working every day with Gus, tucked his new pulp fiction magazine, *Amazing Stories*, under his pillow and sat in bed snuggled under the covers with the Sunday comics section. He wanted to reread about his heroes. Buck Rogers was his absolute favorite, but Tarzan, Flash Gordon, Green Arrow, and Dick Tracy were all close seconds. How he would love to be brave and fearless like they were. Another favorite was Popeye. Popeye had bulging muscles and could lick anybody just by eating spinach. Lou made a mental note to eat more spinach. By the time he got to Lil Abner, he could barely keep his eyes open. As much as he idolized Fearless Fosdick, the comic within the Lil Abner strip, he usually felt more like Joe Btfsplk, the hapless character in Dogpatch who continually had a dark cloud looming over his head. When he could no longer keep his eyes open, he let the newspaper drop to the floor, removed his glasses, and turned off the light.

Sometime during the night, Lou awoke, his breath coming in short gasps and his heart beating fast. He fumbled for the light switch, turned it on, and quickly scanned the room. No one was there and nothing seemed out of place. His model airplanes still flew from the ceiling and his train sat idle on its track. He decided he must have had that dream again, so he switched off the light and wiggled back under the blankets. Closing his eyes, a whisp of a memory flew by, but no matter how hard he tried to catch it, it was gone in an instant. All he could remember was that he'd been chasing something, something always out of his reach. "Someday," he muttered, "I'm going to find out just what it is that I can't get."

In the morning Laura looked up as Lou walked into the kitchen. "Boy, honey, you look like you had a rough night. How late did you stay up reading?"

"Not long, Mom. I just didn't sleep too well."

"Do you feel okay? Are you sick?" She headed toward him, her hand ready to feel his forehead.

Lou pushed her away. "I'm fine. Quit fussing over me."

Laura nuzzled his neck. "Never will I stop fussing over you! You're my baby."

"Mom! I'm twelve! I'm no baby. Stop it!"

Laura smiled and set his breakfast in front of him. "Then eat your oatmeal, sir, before you get too old and lose all your teeth."

Lou couldn't help but giggle.

Lou's English teacher said she had an interesting assignment for her students. "I want you to write a short story with a moral. We'll be giving these stories to the first-grade class. You'll have a week to work on them."

Lou took out a blank piece of paper and stared at it. He looked around the room and saw some students already writing furiously. He wished he had that kind of inspiration. What could he write about? He barely knew what a moral was, much less how to write a story about one.

That night while sitting on his bed, Lou looked around his room for inspiration. When he glanced down at his train set, an idea came to him. He picked up his pencil and started writing and before long his story, *The Caboose That Wanted to be an Engine*, came together. He wrote:

Once upon a time, a yellow caboose named Charlie was part of a train that had a big blue engine and five grey freight cars. Every day the engineer stepped up into Big Blue, the engine, and started down the track. The freight cars followed, with the caboose bringing up the rear.

One day Charlie cautiously approached Big Blue and said, "I'm tired of always being at the end of the train. You're so strong, you get to see everything first, go everywhere first. Wherever I go, I'm the last one to get there."

The engine listened for a moment and said, "What do you want me to do about it? You have to be big and strong to pull this train, that's why I'm in front."

Charlie frowned. "I don't like being the smallest. Even the freight cars are bigger than I am. There's nothing good about being the last car on the train."

Big Blue thought a moment, then said, "I'm not sure that's true, Charlie. I'm the first to go into the unknown. Some of the hills I start down are scary, but being first, I have to go whether I want to or not. And I don't want to tell you how nervous I get going through those long dark tunnels. I have to believe there's blue sky on the other end."

Charlie looked at the engine with more respect. "So, you're saying I never have to be afraid because you've already cleared the way for me?"

"Yeah, boy, that's what I'm saying."

"Oh. I guess it's like being the youngest in a family. You don't get to do anything first, but you know you're protected by the bigger ones who went ahead of you."

"You got it," said Big Blue with a smile, a long whistle, and a puff of smoke.

Chapter Twelve

Lou ran in the house waving his story in the air. In the upper right-hand corner sat a big red A. Laura gave Lou a huge hug and said, "Well look at that! I'm putting this right on the Frigidaire!"

Lou took the paper back and said, "Okay, but first I wanna show Gus" and ran out of the house.

Lou found Gus in the garage with his head under the hood of a car. "Whatcha doing Mr. Gus?"

Gus straightened up and wiped his greasy hands on a nearby towel. A smudge of grease on his face made Lou think of war paint. Gus said, "I'm just trying to get this old lady running again so she can hang on for a few more years. Go start 'er up."

Lou jumped in the car and turned the key. "Nothing happened, now what do I do?"

"Push that starter button on the floor with your foot."

Lou pushed the button and jumped back when the car came to life. Then a grin spread across his face. "Wow, Mr. Gus, don't that beat all?"

"It sure does, son. Looks like we make a good team; we got this little lady up and running fer our customer." Gus closed the hood and told Lou to "shut 'er off."

Lou ran around to the front of the car. "That was fun, Mr. Gus! Someday you'll show me what you did under the hood?"

"I 'spect. What's that paper you got there?"

Lou handed Gus his story. "I got an A on a story I wrote for English class. Mom's gonna put it on the fridge!"

Gus reached in his shirt pocket for his glasses and sat on a paint can to read. Lou studied his face for any sign of approval or disapproval as he read.

Finally, Gus smiled. "Son, that's about the best story I've read in years."

"Really, Mr. Gus? You mean it?"

"Ya. And I wonder if you'd mind writing it again so I can have it to read to my kids. My little one, Eric, is always saying it's not fair that his two brothers get to do things he can't. Yes sir, this story will tell him the things I've been trying to say, only this says it better. Would you do that for me?"

"I'd be real happy to, Mr. Gus."

That night when Emma went to the fridge to get milk, she noticed the story and asked Lou about it. He told her about the assignment and what Gus had said. Emma called to Anna to come and see what their brother had written. After reading the story, Anna asked, "So am I Big Blue?"

"Wait just a minute," said Emma, "what makes you think you're Big Blue? Maybe I am."

"Because I'm older than you," said Anna with a smirk.

"Yeah, by five whole minutes."

"Still, I was born first and let you know it was okay to join me. So see, I'm Big Blue." She turned to Lou. "Right, Charlie the Caboose?"

Lou listened to his sisters arguing back and forth over his story and beamed knowing he'd written something that got people thinking. *Maybe* that's *what a moral is,* he thought.

Chapter Thirteen

The twins ran into the house after school, each girl carrying a bundle. "Mom!" called Emma.

Laura was at the stove taking an apple pie out of the oven. She placed it gently on a hot mat, then turned to Emma. "Hi, girls, whatcha got there?"

Emma set her bundle on the table and Anna did the same. They opened them slowly in an effort to work up a bit of suspense. Anna then grabbed the folded material and shook it out to display a skirt. "See, Mom! We finished our skirts in Home Ec!" Anna was all smiles as she proudly showed off her handiwork. Emma did the same with her skirt, then they laid them side by side.

"Well, I'll be," said Laura. "These look very nice! And to think, you made them yourselves. Go try them on, I want to see them on you." The girls grabbed their skirts and ran up to their room.

Soon they were back in the kitchen, twirling and curtseying and showing off their sewing skills. Laura felt the fabric, examined the waistband and hem on each, and said, "My, you even put in a zipper! I'm impressed. I can't exactly put them on the fridge to show them off, but I can't wait for your dad to see them."

Emma looked at Anna, "Let's keep them on and go work at the office now. We can show Dad while we work." The girls took off running down the street.

When they arrived inside Dyson's Cadillacs, they saw Lou coming toward them, his hands outstretched and covered with grease. "Let me hug you, girls," he said with a wide grin.

The girls shrieked and ran into the office and quickly closed the door while Lou stood outside bent over in laughter. It was so easy to rile girls. They never like to get dirty, especially his sisters. He turned and saw Gus motion to him and hightailed it to the garage.

"Come here, boy," said Gus, "it's time you learned how to change a tire, ya?"

Lou's eyes got big as he realized he was going to learn something new, something real mechanics do. "All right, Mr. Gus, where do we start?"

Gus held up a strange looking item. "See this?"

"Uh huh. What is it?"

"This is called a jack. We use it to raise the car before we can take the tire off."

"Awright! How do we do that?" Lou ran to the car to try and find a place to put the jack.

"Hold on, son, first I need you to wipe your hands, then get inside the car and put the hand brake on."

Lou did as he was told and pulled on the hand brake. "Now what?"

He stepped out of the car and watched Gus put the jack under the bumper and crank a lever up and down. Suddenly, the car was rising off the floor. "Wowee!" cried Lou, "that's amazing."

"See that wrench on the workbench? Bring it here. Now, we need to remove the hub cap and loosen these here nuts." Gus loosened one and handed the wrench to Lou.

Lou put the wrench on, it slipped off; he tried again and this time it held. He put all his weight on the wrench, turning it in the same direction as Gus had, until he felt the nut loosen. Lou's face lit up with the thrill of victory as he smiled at Gus.

"That's good, son, but you've got more. Don't stop now."

Lou put the wrench on the next nut and this time it held the first time. When he finished loosening all the nuts, he said, "What now, Mr. Gus?"

Gus showed him how to remove the nuts and place them in the hub cap for safekeeping. "Now, we can pull this tire right off, you see, and put the spare tire on." Gus pulled off the tire and set it off to the side. "Bring me the spare tire over there and put it on the axle."

Lou brought the tire over and although he had no idea what an axle was, slid the tire into the spot vacated by the old tire.

"Very good," said Gus, giving the tire a spin. "Now put these nuts back in, and tighten them by hand, then with the wrench."

Lou did what Gus said. "Now do we put the hub cap back on?"

"Ya, that's exactly what we do. Go ahead, pop it on."

Lou put the hub cap on and Gus lowered the vehicle with the jack. When the car was firmly on the shop floor, Gus said, "There's one more thing to do; this here tire needs air and," pointing to a spot on the tire, "this stem is where we put it."

"How do we do that, Mr. Gus? Should I blow into it?"

Gus laughed until he had to wipe his eyes. When he was able to talk again, he said, "No, son, we have an easier way to do that job." Gus walked over to the air hose and pulled it toward the wheel.

When he took the cap off the stem, Lou heard a hissing sound and jumped back. "What's that?"

"Just a little air escaping before we put more air in."

"How much air do we put in, Mr. Gus?"

"Cars are different, but this one requires 40 pounds."

Lou's eyes grew big. "Forty pounds? That's an awful lotta air!"

"Forty pounds of pressure, not forty actual pounds. Watch that gauge and tell me when it hits four-oh."

Lou talked all during dinner about how to change a tire. He was animated, waving his fork in the air as he explained to his family about tire jacks, hub caps, nuts, and air hoses. His sisters could care less; they were more interested in keeping their new skirts clean.

Chapter Fourteen

"Whatcha doing, Mama?" asked Lou, watching his mother crisscross pieces of dough on top of an apple pie. Supper was over and Lou and Laura were alone in the kitchen, enjoying a little one-on-one time.

"I'm baking this pie for the fair tomorrow," said Laura, deftly crimping the edges together with her thumb and fingers.

"Ya think you'll win again this year?"

"I hope so, but the competition gets stiffer every year. I might not bring home the blue ribbon tomorrow." Laura put the pie in the oven and closed the door.

Pretty soon the aroma of hot apple pie brought the rest of the family into the kitchen. They each pulled up a chair at the table. Anna absently ran her finger through the flour covering a portion of the table. "I can't believe the fair's tomorrow; I wait all year for it!"

"So do I," said Laura. "I've been going to the county fairs ever since I was four when my parents took me to the biggest fair of all, the World's Fair. I don't remember much, but I do remember I had the most wonderful time in the world!"

Emma asked, "What do you remember the most?"

Laura leaned against the sink, wiped her hands on her apron, and looked past all of them, back to 1904. "It was held in St. Louis, Missouri. It was a long way to go, but my mother and father scrimped and saved for a year to be able to get us there by train. I guess they knew it would be the trip of a lifetime, one we'd always remember.

"The main thing I remember is there were hundreds of thousands of people everywhere. In fact, the newspaper later said that twenty million people attended that year. All I could see were knees and skirts surrounding me everywhere I went, but I could feel the excitement in the air. And the smells, oh, the smells of all that food being sold on the midway."

"That couldn't be much fun," said Lou, "being in a huge crowd of people and not being able to see anything."

"Oh, but it was. At times, my father would pick me up and put me on his shoulders, then I could see everything. I even saw Geronimo!"

Lou was now wide-eyed. "Really? Geronimo the Indian?"

"Yes, sweetheart, the Indian. I saw Thomas Edison, too, even though I didn't realize back then just how important he was. But they did have a building called the Electricity Palace and at night it was all lit up, brighter than anything you've ever seen. Oh, it was beautiful!"

"Wow!" said Lou.

"And believe it or not, I saw the Liberty Bell. They'd carted it to St. Louis just for the Fair."

"No kidding?" said Mike. "You actually saw the Liberty Bell? In person, so to speak?"

"I did, but mostly I remember my parents telling me I saw it. We also had a new treat called an ice cream cone, which isn't new to you kids now, but it sure was then. Another new treat they introduced was cotton candy. I can still taste the sweet sugar."

Lou licked his lips. "I love cotton candy."

"Me, too. So, you can see how my love affair with fairs got started and I've never gotten over it. My best friend, Gracie, and I used to go to the local fairs just to eat the food and ride the Ferris Wheel. Oh, they had a monstrous one at the St. Louis Fair but Mother and Father wouldn't let me ride it."

Anna spoke up. "And now you don't just go to a county fair, Mom, you enter a pie every year and come home with a blue ribbon. I'm proud of you."

"Thank you, sweetie, but I haven't won this year yet. Gracie wins with her pickles every year; we'll get to see her tomorrow." Laura glanced up. "Look at the time, you kids better get to bed and get a good night's sleep. Tomorrow will be a long busy day."

Soon Mike and Laura were alone at the table. Mike said, "I figure if we leave here at nine tomorrow, we'll get there when the gates open and you can drop your pie off with the judges."

In the morning, the five Dysons were on the road, brimming with eager anticipation of the day's events. Sundays, Christmas, Thanksgiving, and Fair Day were the only days of the year that Mike hung a closed sign on his showroom door. While the three children in the back seat sang off key to Meet Me in St. Louis, Louis, Laura gripped the wax paper-covered pie balanced on her lap.

The children stumbled into the house, half asleep yet glowing from their day at the fair. Mike and Laura kissed them goodnight and watched them slowly make their way upstairs. Laura placed her blue ribbon on the counter and lovingly stroked it. A thrill rose inside her, turning her into a four-year-old again.

Monday, after school, Lou ran into the repair shop yelling, "Mr. Gus, did you go to the fair Saturday?"

Gus pulled his head out from under a hood and straightened up. "Ya, took the whole family."

"Did they like it? Cause I sure did. I rode the Ferris Wheel and threw darts at a balloon and won a little stuffed bear and ate cotton candy and had a hot dog with mustard and relish and Mama won first prize for her pie, and . . .."

"Whoa! Sounds like you did just about everything. My young 'uns enjoyed it, too. We didn't win no blue ribbons, but my wife did win a red ribbon for a flower arrangement."

"Huh?"

"That means she took second place. I'm mighty proud of her. She's sickly, you know, so being able to get out and win a ribbon means a lot to her."

"I'm sorry, Mr. Gus, I didn't know she was sick."

"Lotsa people don't know, we don't advertise it none. When she's feeling good, she takes care of our three boys; otherwise, they take care of her."

"What's she got, Mr. Gus?"

"Don't rightly know. She coughs a lot. I'll get her to a doctor one of these days when we can afford it. For now, she loves Hope, her canary, and being able to work in her flower garden. Says she feels close to Heaven when she's out there. Coming on winter, though, so she'll be inside a lot more." Gus wiped his nose. "Enough of this chit chat, get in and start up this here car for me."

Lou spent the rest of the afternoon with his head under the hood of a car, learning how and where to add liquids, and thinking about the fair and cotton candy and Gus' wife. With so many thoughts running through his mind, his emotions rose and fell like a roller coaster.

Chapter Fifteen

"Mr. Gus!"

"Over here, Lou. What's up?"

"We had a Halloween party at school today and had to dress up."

"Ya? Is that your costume you've got on, or did you get kidnapped by a Indian family?"

Lou laughed. "It's my costume. Mom took some feathers from an old hat of hers and sewed them to this piece of cloth for a head band."

"Looks good, but did ya know you got dirt on your face?"

"No I don't, it's war paint; my sisters put it on for me. Don't ya like it?"

"Ya, I do. How about helping me get done early, Chief, so I can get home and help my wife get ready for Halloween. She wants to have the kids bob for apples tonight with blindfolds on. You ever do that?"

"Yup, when I was a kid. It's hard to get an apple without using your hands; ya get a snoot full of water and no apple!" Lou shook his head, remembering water up his nose. "So, what are we doing today?"

"We've got a buyer for one of the cars, so we're gonna put gas in her, then give her a good wax job." Gus went out back and brought a yellow 1935 Cadillac around, then showed Lou how to fill it with gas.

Once the car was washed, they grabbed two towels and a can of wax and worked together on the vehicle. When they were finished, Lou stood back and whistled, "Gee, it looks pretty as a lemon drop."

Gus had to agree that the car looked inviting. "Good job, Chief. What d'ya say we call it a day?"

Lou put his feathered head band back on and raised one hand. "Me go home now. See family. You go home too. See family." Lou then turned and ran out the door, leaving Gus laughing at his protégé.

When Lou walked in the house, he saw a large pumpkin sitting on newspapers on the kitchen table.

"Wowee! Mom. What's going on?"

"This is for you and your sisters to make the scariest jack o'lantern ever. Here's a knife you can use and I think you'll find a candle stub in the drawer."

Lou called upstairs, "Anna, Emma, come down here!"

The girls ran into the kitchen and Emma breathlessly asked, "What is it? Is something wrong?"

"No," said Lou. "Mom got us this pumpkin to carve. You girls can draw the face and I'll scoop out the insides."

"Is that all you called us down here for? We're too old for such childish stuff," Anna huffed.

"Right," said Emma, "but since we're here, we might as well do the shrimp a favor and at least show him how to draw a face." Emma picked up a pencil and drew a circle for an eye.

"Not like that," said Anna, taking the pencil from her. "It's supposed to be a triangle, like this. See?"

"Oh yeah. Do the nose like that, too. Now do the mouth."

Lou watched as his sisters, who were too old for such childish stuff, stood over the pumpkin engrossed in the task of drawing a face.

When Anna finished drawing the mouth, Lou saw that it had a wide grin with a few teeth here and there.

"Thanks, I can take it from here, guys," said Lou, "I'll just cut along the lines you made." Lou picked up the knife and sliced off the top of the pumpkin, leaving the stem and strings of pumpkin hanging from it. Then he scooped out the goo and seeds and, with his hands dripping with gunk, threatened to hug his sisters until they ran out of the room screaming. Chuckling, Lou washed his hands then proceeded to cut out the eyes and nose, following Anna's lines.

Hunched over the table, he was fully absorbed in carefully cutting around a tooth when he heard a loud "Boo!" that startled him and made him jump. The knife slipped and cut into the tooth, leaving a jagged, gaping hole in the pumpkin's mouth.

Lou heard his sisters giggling and was ready to pounce on them in anger until he looked at his jack o'lantern and saw it was now scarier than before. He calmed down and said, "You didn't scare me none; I jumped so's you'd think you did."

"Sure," said Emma. "We scared you and you know it. Put the candle in; let's see it lit up."

Lou set the candle firmly inside the pumpkin, lit it, and put the top back on so the stringy residue cast an eerie look to the face.

Laura entered the kitchen and cried out at the mess, but when she saw the pumpkin leering at her, she softened her tone and complimented her children on their artistry. She then picked the seeds out of the gunk and washed them off so they could be salted, roasted, and eaten. "Lou, honey, clean off the table so the girls can set it for dinner."

Lou balled up the newspapers with the pumpkin's innards and dropped them in the waste basket. Then he picked up the jack o'lantern and carried it toward the front door to put it on the step just as Mike walked in.

"Well, look at that!" said Mike. "Did you do that, Lou?"

"Yup, with a little help from the girls." Lou walked past his father to get outside. When the screen door slammed behind him, he lurched forward and dropped the pumpkin. It smashed against the cement step. Lou dropped to the step and picked up the stem. As the tears fell, he threw back his arm and flung the stem and top into the street, then ran over and stomped on it.

Mike came outside and saw Lou in the street and the shattered jack o'lantern on the step. He walked over to Lou and held him for a few moments, then they picked up the stem and came back to the step. "What happened, son?"

Lou sobbed. "I dropped it. I can't do anything right."

Mike handed him a handkerchief. "Accidents happen, Lou. You didn't throw it down on purpose, did you?"

"No, but I mess up everything I do. I'm just a jinx. Do ya think I'll ever be able to do anything right like Larry would've?"

Mike smiled at his son. "You're not Larry, you're Lou. And I happen to love Lou. Clean up this mess and go inside while I go to the car lot and make sure the cars don't get soaped tonight. By the way, I got to see your jack o'lantern and it looked real good. Remember, every day is a new day with new opportunities."

Sure, thought Lou. *New opportunities to mess up. I need you, Larry; I need my brother.*

Chapter Sixteen

By the end of the 1936 school year, Anna and Emma had each made a dress with a matching cape. They were both made from the same pattern and both used a flowered print. The flowers on Anna's dress were blue and on Emma's they were green, opposite of their favorite colors to show the world they had broken out of the twin mold.

Lou had a growth spurt that added two inches to his height and his voice was deeper, most of the time. Gus had taught him how to change the oil and do basic car services. He could now handle a lube job with ease, mount and change a tire, and replace belts and spark plugs. One day Gus told Lou, "Chief, I gotta say you're a natural when it comes to mechanics, ya?" Lou beamed.

On the last day of school, when the final bell rang, Lou ran home, let the kitchen screen door bang, and called, "Hi Mom." Getting no answer, he walked toward the living room and quickly stopped. Gus was pacing, looking worried and speaking in hushed tones to Mike and Laura.

Laura looked up and saw Lou, smiled, and wordlessly indicated he should go up to his room. A short time later, Lou heard a door close and looked out his bedroom window in time to see Gus walk back toward the garage. Lou ran downstairs and found his parents crying.

"Mom?" Lou tentatively asked. "What's going on? Is something wrong with Mr. Gus?"

Laura wiped her eyes and blew her nose. "No, dear. It's his wife. He says she's been sick for quite a while—"

"I know."

"Well, he took her to a doctor yesterday and he told them she has TB."

"What's TB?"

"Tuberculosis. It's a very dangerous and contagious disease."

"Can they give her medicine?"

"I'm afraid there's nothing they can do for her," said Mike. "Sunshine is her best medicine. Now that school is out, you'll need to spend more time at the garage to help Gus."

Can I go see him now?"

"Sure."

Lou ran to the garage, then slowed as he entered the shop. Gus was sitting there methodically wiping his tools and setting them back down one at a time. He appeared to be in a daze. When he saw Lou, he forced a smile and nodded. "Hi, Chief."

"Hi, Mr. Gus. I'm sorry about your wife."

Gus stopped what he was doing and motioned to Lou to sit down. "I'm proud of you, son, you've come a long way since you started here last fall. I'm afraid I'm going to need you more than ever for a while, ya?"

69

"Anything. Just tell me what you want me to do."

Gus turned his head for a moment and made a quick swipe at his nose. Turning back to Lou, he said, "I've talked with your dad and you two will take over the garage for a few weeks so I can take my wife up ta the Cape to see if rest and sun will help 'er."

"Wow, Mr. Gus! I'm happy for me and Dad, but sad for you and your wife. Are ya boys going with you?"

"No, Lou. TB is very contagious so the boys are staying with my sister until it's safe for them to come home again."

"Aren't ya afraid you'll catch it?"

"Well, that's a chance I have to take. I'm not leaving her alone. If Cape Cod doesn't do the work, then she'll have to go into a sanitarium and I won't be able to visit her at all."

"Gosh! That'd be awful."

"Ya, well uh, let's get busy and get the major work done today. Rose is home packing and we'll be leaving in the morning. Think you and your dad can handle things while I'm gone?"

"Piece of cake. It'll be swell to work with my dad for a while."

That night around the supper table, talk centered on Gus and Rose. Mike passed a bowl of peas to Lou and said, "Looks like I'm putting my mechanics coveralls on again. I hope I remember what Gus taught me; it's been a while."

70

"It'll come back to ya, Dad. I'll help ya."

Emma asked, "Will that affect what we do in the office?"

Mike smiled. "I'm glad you asked. You girls are going to be promoted to sales staff, plus keeping the office running."

"Really? We get to sell cars?"

"Think you can?"

"Well yeah. We've answered enough phone calls to learn to deal with the public, and we've filed enough invoices to understand prices, models, and selling points. If we *should* have a problem, you'll help us, won't you?"

"Of course. But you may have to let me wash my hands first!"

Chapter Seventeen

The next morning, the entire Dyson family walked over to Dyson's Cadillacs and entered the employee entrance, ready to work as a team to keep the business running during Gus' absence. After turning the lights on in the showroom, Mike offered up a quick prayer for strength and wisdom for each family member as they prepared to tackle their new tasks.

Mike took Emma and Anna into the office and showed them where to find new car sales forms and how to figure the sales tax. Then he took them to the showroom floor and explained the particular unique features of three of the cars. Mike lovingly stroked the curved fender of a maroon Fleetwood Cadillac. "Now this V-12 convertible has three-speed synchromesh transmission, independent front suspension with coil springs, a floating rear axle—"

"Dad," said Anna, "we can't remember all that. Isn't it written somewhere?"

Mike chuckled, "Yeah, I suppose it is. If a customer wants to know the inner workings of any of these cars, come and get me. Okay?"

Emma relaxed. "Okay. Thanks."

Mike and Laura walked into the garage where Lou was already reading a note Gus had left for him.

"Dad, Gus left us a schedule of the repairs that need to be done. Some of these are pretty minor that I can do, but the others are up to you. I've seen Gus do some of these jobs, but I don't know how he did them so get your coveralls on and let's get to work."

Mike looked at Laura and smiled at the way their little boy had grown up. Laura said, "I'm leaving you guys alone before you ask me to change a tire. Okay if I wash the showroom windows and do general housekeeping in there?"

Mike nodded. "That'd be great, hon."

Laura entered the showroom from the garage with a spring in her step because for the first time, she was actively involved in the family business. She went into the bathroom to get a bucket and rag and made a mental note that the bathroom definitely needed to be cleaned once the showroom windows were washed. She heard the clang of a tool dropping on the cement floor and beamed, knowing her husband and son were bonding like never before.

In the garage, Mike wriggled into Gus' coveralls while Lou picked up the jack handle he'd dropped and proceeded to change a tire. Mike thought how competent his son looked, although he knew Lou well enough to know that inside Lou felt anything but competent in most matters. *What a shame,* Mike thought. *He has a lot to offer if he only realized how good he is.*

Mike picked up Gus' list and was relieved to learn there were only two major jobs that needed his attention. The first was a brake job. Once the car was jacked up safely and the tires removed, Mike laid on Gus' handmade wooden creeper and slid under the car. "Get down here, son, I want you to learn how to do a

73

brake job. We need to change the shoes and lubricate the drums."

Lou dropped down to the hard floor and eased himself under the car next to his father. "This is fun, ain't it Dad?"

"Yeah, sure. I'll be happy when Gus gets back, though. It's been a long time since I've gotten under a car."

"I sure hope Gus' wife gets better, don't you Dad?"

"I do, son."

For the next hour Lou watched his dad work on the brakes and occasionally had to wipe drops of grease off his face. When they finished, they stood and stretched. "Good job, son. Now put the tires back on and I'll take it for a test drive, then we can let Mr. Blakely know he can have his car back."

After a lunch delivered by Laura, Mike said, "Our next job is to replace Ruth Wilson's windshield. I'll bring her car in."

When the '32 red and white Roadster convertible entered the garage, Lou shook his head at the shattered windshield and asked, "What happened to her car?"

Mike exited the car and brushed glass shards off the front seat. "She told me she was parked on the road in front of her house and when she came out to go to church, her windshield was smashed. When she looked in the car, a baseball was sitting on her front seat."

"Did she find out who did it?"

"She has her suspicions, but nothing definite. What d'ya say we fix this for her so she can have her car back. This is the second time I've replaced a windshield for her. The first time was when a tree branch came down in a storm. That old lady's just bad luck when it comes to cars. She should've stuck with her horse, Bandit. We didn't have to replace anything on him!"

At supper that night, the girls were all aglow as they talked about a customer who had come in. "I showed him the maroon Fleetwood, Dad," said Emma, "and he said he really liked it. I didn't even have to tell him all that other stuff you said. He just sat in the driver's seat, and smiled while he stroked the dashboard."

"And," Anna chimed in, "he said he might be back this week if he can find the money to buy it. Can you believe it? We may have sold our first car?"

"Good girls!" Mike exclaimed. "You two may have found your life's calling. As for me, I left work dirty and tired, but it felt real good to put in a hard day of honest labor." He smiled at Lou. "And, I did it side by side with my son."

Lou nodded and smiled, but his eyes were having trouble staying open. Working a full day was far more taxing than working a few hours after school.

Chapter Eighteen

For the entire month of July, the Dysons worked in tandem to keep the showroom and garage running smoothly. The more Mike worked in the garage, the more he longed for the time he would be back in the showroom in a suit and tie and clean fingernails. But he knew he would miss working with Lou when Gus returned. He and Lou had kept the shop running smoothly and gotten to know each other on a deeper level than ever before. He could see Lou developing in confidence and ability more each day as Lou took over running the garage and assigning work schedules.

In the office, the twins had settled in to their new job. As people called to schedule a repair, the girls gave them a slot of time and by now were able to estimate how long the job would take. Each day they prepared a list of needed repairs and presented it to Lou. Their high moment came when the customer came back and bought the new maroon Fleetwood he had looked at earlier. They ran into the garage and got Mike to meet the gentleman and to make sure they'd done everything right. In addition, they'd sold a couple of used Cadillacs to eager buyers. After each sale, the kids and Mike walked in the house after work to the enticing aroma of a cake in the oven. Laura celebrated each sale with her Depression cake with peanut butter frosting.

On August tenth, Mike and Lou were bent over a car with their heads under the hood listening to the motor when they heard a familiar voice say, "Sounds good, ya?"

"Gus is back!" shouted Lou as he ran over to hug him, but stopped short so as not to get Gus' street clothes dirty.

Gus held a paper bag out to Lou. "It's not much, this Depression and all, but I got ya some salt water taffy for your birthday. Thirteen now are ya? Seems like you grew a couple a inches since I left. And your voice has gotten a bit lower, too."

Lou laughed. "Thanks Mr. Gus!" He unwrapped a piece of candy and popped it in his mouth.

Mike slammed the hood, wiped his hands, and walked toward Gus, grinning. "Sure is good to see ya, Gus. How's Rose? Did the rest and sun help?"

Gus looked at the cement floor. "No sir, 'fraid not. Her doctor's getting a bed ready for her at the sanitarium. She's at the house in bed now. I'll probably be taking her to the home tomorrow."

Mike hung his head. "I'm so sorry, Gus. If there's anything we can do to help, just say the word."

"Thanks, boss."

Lou asked, "Are your boys home now?"

"No, Chief, it's not safe yet. They can come home after she goes . . .." Gus turned his back and tried, without success, to stifle a sob. "I gotta go. I'll be back at work day after tomorrow."

"Of course, Gus. Take whatever time you need."

Gus walked to his car without turning around.

Lou looked at his dad. "That's so sad. I wish we could do something for him."

Mike lifted the car's hood again. "In a case like this, the only thing we can do is pray for Rose. Can you do that?"

"Sure. But I 'spect the doctors know what they're doing."

"It never hurts to go right to the top, son. Hand me that wrench."

True to his word, two days later a subdued Gus entered the garage, donned his coveralls, and checked the day's schedule, a cigarette in one hand and a cup of coffee in the other. Lou and Mike arrived and on seeing Gus, broke into a wide smile. "Ah," said Mike, "looks like I can stay in my good clothes today. Let me bring you up to date, then I'll go to the showroom and help the girls. I'm happy to say business is picking up a bit."

"Good to hear it, boss."

While Lou set about changing a tire, Mike noticed the vacant look in Gus' eyes. "She settled in?" he asked tentatively.

"Ya, it's a decent room, not great, but if it helps her, it'll be worth it."

"I'm sorry, Gus. I don't know what else to say."

"I know. I'm doing all I can not to lose hope; it's all I got left."

"She'll get better; I know she will. Are your boys home?"

"I'm getting 'em tonight. Last night I disinfected the house to get it ready for 'em. Last thing I want is for m'boys to get sick."

"Come over for supper tonight; Laura would love to have you join us."

"Don't mind if I do. Home cooking sounds good." Gus turned and watched Lou put the new tire on. "You've got a good boy, there, boss. He'll have me out of a job in no time."

"Don't plan on it, Gus. No one can replace you. We've just had six weeks to find that out. Truth is," Mike laughed, "we found it out the first week."

Gus stubbed out his cigarette. "Guess I'll go help the boy."

Chapter Nineteen

In the weeks that followed, Gus came in early so he could have time at the end of his work day to ride over to the sanitarium to see Rose. His sister had come to watch the boys and help with the housecleaning. Since he could only wave to Rose from the parking lot as she watched from an upstairs window, Gus sometimes brought the boys with him. Seeing them brought a smile to her face. At times, they would hold up a sign saying I LOVE YOU or I MISS YOU MOM and they'd see their mother wipe her eyes.

Rose and Gus had three boys, Eric eight, Karl fifteen, and Gus Jr. seventeen. Rose had had two miscarriages between Karl and Eric that took a lot out of her. Eric was a blessing, but after he was born, they took steps not to take any more chances with Rose's life. Gus and Rose raised their boys to be bright, independent, and hardworking young men.

Gus was well aware of the possibility that he might have to finish raising the boys by himself, but he kept those thoughts hidden in his heart. Alone at night with God, he felt free to release his feelings and frustrations. *Why? Why her? She never hurt a flea, God; she loved you and we always thought you loved her, too. So why don't you heal her and bring her back to me and the boys? I'll do anything you want; just tell me what it is you want me to do.*

Mike could see the worry lines on Gus' face each morning at work, but tried to deflect the situation by talking about anything but Rose. Sometimes it helped, usually it didn't.

In the following two weeks, Gus took Lou under his wing and showed him how to take a transmission apart and put it back together. Lou was ecstatic. He was about to enter eighth grade and he just knew that school couldn't possibly be as interesting as what he was learning with Gus. During a coffee break one day, Lou approached Gus for his advice.

"Mr. Gus, I've been thinking about school starting next week."

Gus lit a cigarette and exhaled a ring of smoke. "Me, too, Chief. Won't be the same working here by m'self."

"That's what I wanna talk to ya about. I can learn more by staying here with you than I can sitting in a boring classroom."

"Are you saying what I'm a thinking you're saying?"

"Yeah. I think I should quit school and apprentice under you. It makes sense to me. What do ya think?"

"Boy, you best not ask what I think 'cause you wouldn't like it."

"But . . .."

"No buts. You're gonna stay in school and learn a lot more than mechanics. Do you wanna do hard labor all your life and see nothing but dirt under your fingernails? This is a good job, son, but you owe it to yourself to learn what else is out there that you might wanna do for a living."

"So you won't talk to my dad for me?"

"Not about this, nosiree. This will be our little secret, a conversation that never happened. Got it?"

"Got it. So I guess I start school next week and work with you after school and on Saturdays."

"Ya, you're a smart boy."

One Sunday afternoon, when Rose had been gone for three months, there was a knock on the Dyson's door. Mike opened the door to see Gus carrying something large.

"Hey Gus, come on in."

Gus took his hat off with his free hand, wiped his feet, and stepped into the house. Laura came into the room and smiled when she saw Gus. Hearing his voice, Lou and the girls ran down the stairs to greet him. "Hi Gus," said Lou, "whatcha got there?"

Gus set down the item he was carrying and whipped off the sheet that was covering it. What the family saw was a bird cage with a little yellow bird inside, sitting on a perch.

"Oh my!" cried Laura. "How sweet!"

Gus hung his head. "I thought you might like it, missus. He was Rose's bird. His name is Hope 'cause we thought it was a female when we got it. I'd like you to have 'im."

Laura knelt down to look at the yellow ball of fluff. The bird started to sing. "Oh! Listen to that! Isn't he beautiful?" Then she looked at Gus. "But, why—"

Gus studied the floor. "My Rose died yesterday. They told me when I got there."

Mike put his arm around Gus' shoulders. Laura went to him and gave him a kiss on his cheek while wiping tears from her own cheeks. The twins ran over and gave him a hug.

Lou let out an anguished cry and ran to Gus. "I'm so sorry Mr. Gus. Is there anything I can do for you?"

Gus swiped his sleeve across his nose and cheek and said, "Ya, be at the shop tomorrow after school. I won't be leaving early . . . any more."

Laura tentatively asked, "Have you had time to think about a funeral? If you don't mind, we'd like to attend."

Gus cleared his throat. "My sister and I and the boys plan to start making arrangements tonight. I'll let ya know when and where to come."

"Thanks Gus," said Laura, "and thanks so much for this adorable little bird. I've always wanted a canary; I'm just sorry I had to get him this way. I'll take good care of Hope and you can visit him anytime you want. Any time at all."

That night suppertime conversation was subdued. While the Dyson's ate in silence, Hope, beginning to adjust to his new surroundings, sang a lilting tune to lift the pall that hung over the room.

Chapter Twenty

Finishing work on a '32 Cadillac, Gus threw the keys to Lou and said, "Let's take er for a test drive."

Lou jerked his head toward Gus. Suddenly his feet were glued to the floor, his eyes bulged and his mouth was locked in the open position. A few seconds later, Lou found his voice and asked, "Ya mean it, Mr. Gus? You're gonna teach me how ta drive?"

"Ya. I've taught m'boys, I 'spect I can teach you. If you want to, that is."

"I do. I do."

"Okay then, get in the driver's seat and I'll be right beside ya."

Lou climbed into the light blue coupe and sat tall in the seat, a king surveying his surroundings.

"Start er up," instructed Gus.

Lou turned the key, pulled out the choke, and pressed the starter button with his foot. "Now what?"

"Now, step on the clutch and put er in first."

Lou clamped his teeth and squinted his eyes in complete concentration. His hand covered the shifting lever; he moved it and a loud grinding sound filled the air. Lou jumped and released his hand and foot and the car stalled.

Gus chuckled. "You're doing good, Chief, for a beginner. Try it again."

Lou started the car again, stepped on the clutch, and moved the shifting lever. There was no grinding sound.

"Good, good," said Gus, "now press lightly on the accelerator. Lightly, I said!"

Lou's foot was busy going back and forth between the accelerator and the brake as the coupe moved forward. The car headed toward the right side of the road so Lou yanked the steering wheel and suddenly he was heading toward the left side.

"It doesn't take much steering ta keep the car straight. Slow and steady, son."

More grinding of gears and a good bit of bucking down the road occurred before Lou had better control over the monster. He was glad Gus had him take a back road where there were no other cars to contend with. Gus had told him to line up the lady on the hood ornament with the center of the road. That advice helped him keep from over steering. Soon Lou could relax, slightly, and allow a smile to crease his face.

By the time they got back to the shop, Lou wore a full-on grin and looked like he had just reached the summit of Mt. Everest. He shut off the car and climbed down, gently closing the door behind him.

Gus got out the other side and said, "Good job. Looks like you were born ta drive."

"Really? Ya think I did alright?"

"Ya."

"I love this car. I want one just like it when I get old enough."

Gus nodded, pushing his blond hair back.

Lou looked up and asked, "Do you mind my asking ya, Mr. Gus, how you got that scar on your face?"

Gus fingered the scar. "Not at all, it might teach ya something." He had Lou's full attention. "Not all cars start like this here Cadillac. Some ya have to crank from the front of the car, but if you don't do it right, well, you can have trouble."

"What kinda trouble?"

"Big trouble. I was cranking a Model T once and bent over to put my whole weight into it. Just as the car started, the crank jerked and didn't it spin and fly right off? It broke m'thumb and cut my face. Doc Lawrence fixed me up. Be careful, boy, if you ever start a car with a crank."

"I will, Mr. Gus. Now I'm gonna go tell my mom and dad that I drove a car today!"

Chapter Twenty-One

September 1937. The Great Depression was still very much in evidence providing no money for trivial pastimes like movies or dances. Not being able to go to dances was a big problem for Laura Dyson. During the Roaring Twenties, and with their young children watching, Laura and Mike won many Charleston contests. Her fringe dress still hung in the back of the closet as a reminder of those happier times. They had even entered a dance marathon one night, but gave up after three hours because of the total insanity of it all. The small cash prize was not worth the torture, nor would it cover a doctor's bill for the damage it would inflict on their feet if they had continued.

With little money and lots of time in the evening, the family spent hours playing Monopoly at the kitchen table. Mike usually ended up with all the money and property, but it was getting harder for him to beat Anna. She was shrewd and had an uncanny knack for wheeling and dealing. Laura was fond of saying, "Looks like you met your match, Mike."

Mike responded one night with, "I can see that! Anna's got a good future ahead if a company can get past the fact that she's a female. She can sell as good as a man any day."

Anna smiled at the praise.

"What about me?" asked Emma. "What am I good at?"

Mike stroked his chin. "Hmm, let me see. I think your talent lies in dressmaking. What do you think, Laura?"

Laura nodded. "I think you're right. There's not a lot of call for dressmaking these days, but since people are trying to make their old clothes last longer, I believe she could make a good living at tailoring and altering. Emma?"

Emma's eyes shone with delight. "That's a good idea and it's something I can do from home. Thanks, Mom."

"And me?" asked Lou.

"You keep doing what you're doing," said Mike, "and you'll find your calling by the time you graduate. It may be repairing cars or it could be something totally different. The one thing I do know is you'll put your whole self into whatever you do."

Laura reached over and patted Lou's arm and kissed the top of his head. He squirmed away, he was too old for such mushy stuff.

"Mom!" Emma called as she ran into the house. It was spring and the twins were seniors at New Haven High.

"I'm in the bathroom. Watch your step, I just mopped the floor."

"Mom, we've got something to tell you; come in the kitchen!"

Laura put the mop down and dried her hands on her apron as she entered the kitchen. "Okay, I'm here. What's up?"

Emma looked at Anna and grinned, then took a deep breath before talking. "We found out today that out of the fifty-four students in our class, we're both in the top ten!"

"And," added Anna, "Emma was named salutatorian! My boyfriend is valedictorian."

Laura clapped her hands. "Oh, girls, I'm so proud of you! It seems like you were just six years old and starting first grade and here you are, graduating high school. And top of the class yet! Wait 'til I tell your father; he'll be so proud. And we're proud of Ned, too."

Anna looked at Emma. "I'm glad I don't have to give a speech at graduation; you can have that honor."

"Thanks," said Emma, "but I'll expect you to help me. You have a way with words that I don't."

Mike, Laura and Lou sat proudly in the audience listening to Emma and Ned give their speeches. When the girls' names were called to receive their diplomas, Lou jumped up and yelled "Hurrah." To celebrate the happy occasion, Mike and Laura treated the family to dinner at Howard Johnson's.

Lou took in all the sights. "Wow, Mom, this is keen! I never thought I'd get to eat in a restaurant."

Emma took a sip of water. "I know what a sacrifice this dinner is for you, Mom and Dad, and I'll never forget this night and what you've done for Anna and me."

"You girls are worth it," said Mike. "So, eat up and enjoy yourselves."

Chapter Twenty-Two

July 12, 1938. To celebrate Lou's fifteenth birthday, his parents rented a boat for a day on Long Island Sound. They brought along a picnic basket carrying a lunch that Laura had packed, consisting of egg and tuna salad sandwiches, cookies straight out of the oven, chips, and drinks. The warm weather and cloudless blue sky provided the ideal backdrop. The boat had an outboard motor and Mike told Lou, "You're good with engines and mechanical things, why don't you take the helm and steer this thing?"

When everyone was seated evenly in the small boat, Lou grabbed the handle and yanked on the cord. He smiled when the engine sputtered and came to life. He slowly steered the boat away from the dock and headed out toward open water. Soon they were gliding along peacefully with the Connecticut shore on their left and the New York shore barely visible on their right. An hour into the trip, Lou shut down the motor and let the boat drift while they ate lunch, talked, and enjoyed the warmth of the sun. They could hear the birds in the trees along the shore. Occasionally, a bass jumped out of the water to snare an unsuspecting bug.

Laura was lulled into a sleepy state. "I'm having a hard time keeping my eyes open," she said. "I feel so full and contented, I could go to sleep right here to the gentle rocking of the boat."

"Me, too," said Lou. "This is the best birthday I've ever had!"

A short time later, a cloud floated overhead, giving a chill when it blocked out the sun. Mike glanced up and said, "Maybe you'd better start the engine, son, I don't like the looks of those dark clouds in the east. Have you noticed that the birds have stopped chattering in the trees? That's not a good sign. We need to start making our way back to shore, storms can come up quickly out here on the water."

Lou started the engine and navigated the boat back toward the direction of the dock. When the dock came in sight but was still some ways off, huge raindrops started pelting them, eliciting a shriek from the girls who put cushions over their heads. Laura put the empty picnic basket over her head while Lou and Mike concentrated on the looming dock and the waves that were now anything but calm.

"Slow and easy, son," cautioned Mike. "Don't hit the dock. A little to the left, now right, that's it." Mike reached for the dock rope while Lou cut the engine. Mike stood and stepped onto the dock to help his family out of the boat. Just as he extended his hand to Laura, a wave crashed, forcefully rocking the boat back and forth. "Hurry up Laura!"

Laura grabbed Mike's hand and quickly scrambled onto the dock. Now the two of them stretched out their arms to help the girls. Anna and Emma stood, but before they could step out, a large wave smashed into the boat and tipped it over. Laura gasped as she and Mike watched their three children tumble into the water.

Above the roar of the rain and waves, Laura yelled, "Quick Mike, do something!" Mike was about to jump in when he saw Lou paddling furiously with one arm and cradling Anna with the other. Mike sprawled across the dock, reached down and grabbed Anna and pulled her up, then handed her to Laura. When he looked back at the water, Lou was no longer visible.

The next few minutes seemed like hours before Lou appeared again, holding onto Emma. Mike reached for her and pulled her to safety while Lou swam toward the shore and crawled out of the water, collapsing on the bank. Emma's leg was bleeding and she coughed up a large amount of water. Mike handed her to Laura, then dove in to turn the boat upright. Lou jumped back into the water to help his father, then they both scrambled to shore, wet and exhausted.

Laura held onto Emma as she hopped her way to the dry car; the rest of the family ran ahead to get out of the rain.

The girls shivered in the back seat under a blanket. "Th . . . th . . . thank you, Lou," said Anna.

Emma added, "Y . . . you may be our little b . . . brother, but today you are our big brave brother!" She coughed and sputtered and added, "I thought I was . . . going to die. I got caught under the boat and the waves . . . kept dashing me . . . against the dock piling. I was so scared. Ow, my leg hurts."

Mike drove home as fast as he could and helped Emma out of the car and into the warm house. "You all get some dry clothes on while I heat some soup to warm our insides. We'll take you to the doctor tomorrow, Emmie. Your leg is cut up pretty bad."

When they were all back in the kitchen and Emma's leg was bandaged, Mike crushed crackers into his tomato soup and said, "That was some good work you did today, Lou. I'm proud of you."

Lou hung his head. "I'm not. Larry would've gotten you back to the dock before the rain came. He would've watched the girls when they stood up to make sure their weight was distributed so the boat didn't tip. He would have done so many things I didn't—"

"Lou!" Mike's voice rose. "We can all go through life saying *what if*, but the fact is, you saved your two sisters' lives. They never learned to swim like you did. Don't think 'what would Larry do;' instead think of your twin brother as your guardian angel who was watching over you today and helped you when you needed it most. Can you do that?"

Lou took a sudden interest in his bowl of soup. "I guess. It was pretty scary when I went back down for Em. I couldn't see anything and I wasn't sure how long I could hold my breath. I was relieved when I went under the boat and felt her hand. I just grabbed it and got out of there as fast as I could."

Anna and Emma got up from the table and smothered Lou with kisses. "Our hero!" they exclaimed.

Lou shooed them away and quickly wiped their kisses off with a napkin. "I'm no hero, heroes don't get scared. I'm just glad we're all okay."

"Amen," chorused the rest of the family.

94

Chapter Twenty-Three

Doctor Hansen told Emma she could go back to the waiting room and sit with Anna and Lou while he talked with her parents. He called Mike and Laura into his office.

"Well, doctor," said Laura, "is her leg going to heal all right?"

The doctor cleaned his glasses on his lab coat before speaking. "I'm afraid the news isn't good. It appears your girl cut her leg on a rusty nail when she crashed against the old wood piling. She has a fever of 104 degrees which tells me she has an infection. I recommend she go into the hospital for a while until we can get the fever and infection under control."

"Oh dear," said Laura. "Of course, we want to do whatever you think is best for her."

"That's right," said Mike. "Did you tell her about the hospital?"

"Not yet, I wanted to ask your permission first."

Laura wiped her eyes. "You have our permission; we want her to get better."

"I'll call the hospital right now and see if they can get her in," said the doctor.

In the waiting room, the five Dysons sat immersed in their own thoughts. They glanced up in unison when the doctor entered. Laura and Mike looked at him pleadingly, not knowing what questions to ask.

"I have good news for you," said Doctor Hansen. "They have a bed available and Emma can go right over now."

"Right now?" asked Laura.

"Yes. The sooner we start treatment, the quicker she'll get better."

Mike helped Emma to the car and when everyone was in, drove to New Haven General. Doctor Hansen met them there and made sure Emma was admitted quickly. Once she was settled in a ward, the doctor took the family aside. "Emma has had a pretty rough day and needs her rest. I suggest you all go home and let us take care of her. You can come back tomorrow afternoon."

At home, no one felt like talking. Anna felt as though half of her body was lying in a bed a few miles away. Lou blamed himself for his sister being there, as though he could have done something, or maybe shouldn't have done something, that caused her to get hurt. Mike and Laura had never had one of their children in a hospital other than when they were born and knowing they were not all together under one roof was unsettling indeed. When Laura heard Hope chirp a cheerful tune in his cage, she smiled even though she was not at all happy.

Lou heard crying coming from Anna's room and went in to see her. He handed her a handkerchief to dry her eyes. "Can I help?" he asked.

"No," Anna sobbed. "You can't possibly understand what I'm going through, having my other half not here."

Lou moved away from her. "Really? You think I don't know what it's like to not have my twin here? I miss Larry every single day. At least you've gotten to know Em, what she looks like, you've heard her voice, seen her grow up. All I know about Larry is he lived for three days. Period." Lou grabbed the handkerchief back to dry his own eyes.

Anna went to Lou and hugged him hard. "I'm so sorry, Louie. I keep forgetting you're a twin, too and must have a lot of the feelings I have except, like you said, you never even got to know your brother. Will you forgive me?"

Lou looked at the floor boards. "I guess." Then he smiled and said, "Aw heck, you know I can never stay mad at you."

The next day Doctor Hansen told Mike and Laura that Emma's fever had gone down some, offering hope in that regard. For her leg, the nurses were applying colloidal silver on the infected area, alternating with poultices. "The best we can do," he said, "is to hope and wait. If you're the praying type, I'd recommend it."

They stopped in Emma's room to see her, but she was sleeping so they kissed her cheek, offered up a prayer, and went home.

Chapter Twenty-Four

For the rest of that summer, Lou took lifeguard lessons. He told his parents he wanted to save as many people as he could from drowning. His mornings were spent working at the garage in coveralls and his afternoons found him at the Sound in swim trunks and sporting a golden tan.

Anna spent more and more time in the office learning all she could about business and marketing. She told her dad, "I just love selling cars and taking care of customers. I feel alive as soon as I walk in the showroom door."

Mike hugged her and said, "I'm glad you feel that way, honey, because you're really good at it. I've noticed you don't try to hard sell the customers. Instead, you let them decide if they can afford a new car or if it's better for them to repair their current car. I see this as a win-win situation for them and us, so keep up the good work."

Anna beamed at the praise.

As often as possible, Laura visited her Emmie in the hospital, hoping to see a spark of improvement. However, each time she came home, the disappointment lay over her like a heavy wool blanket. Emma's ward was a depressing place. Eight women occupied the room, all admitted for a range of illnesses from polio to ulcers. At times, the noise from the moaning and screams caused Laura to bolt out of the room and seek solace in the waiting room. *I don't know how Emmie can stand it. I would go crazy if I had to stay here very long. It appears my daughter is a lot stronger than I ever gave her credit for.*

After three more weeks, the doctor allowed Mike and Laura to bring Emma home with strict instructions on how to take care of her leg. Laura was ecstatic to get her daughter out of that dismal ward. Anna jumped with joy when she saw the car pull in and her parents help Emma into the house. Her other half was at last home where she belonged.

That night when Lou returned from his lifeguard lesson, he felt a happiness in the house that hadn't been there in a long time. His suspicions were confirmed when he saw the sheer joy on everyone's face. He ran upstairs to the twin's bedroom and broke into a wide grin when he saw Emma. They hugged each other for a long time before he let her lie back down and rest. Things weren't perfect at the Dyson household, but they were certainly a lot better now that they were all together again. Just having her home was good medicine for the entire family.

As Emma gained strength, she made her way downstairs more often. She couldn't wait to join the world and feel part of her family again. Eventually, she carved a spot for herself on the sofa with a footstool for her leg and an end table beside her to hold her sewing supplies. Little by little, word got out to her friends and their families that there was a seamstress available for alterations and repairs. The money that Emma brought in was helpful, but the greatest benefit of her enterprise was the satisfaction it brought to her, knowing she wasn't a helpless invalid. One afternoon she looked at the woman's blouse on her lap that needed mending and told Laura, "I can suffer through anything, Mom, as long as I know I'm a contributing member of this family. I couldn't imagine being bed-ridden the rest of my life."

Laura nodded, looked upwards, and mouthed the words, *Thank you.*

In September, Lou began his sophomore year in high school. The economy was improving slightly; there was a glimmer of hope in the air about the future. Anna was kept busy in the office as more and more customers brought their cars in for repair now that they could afford to. She even sold a few new cars, much to her and her family's delight.

Doctor Hansen stopped by every week to check on Emma's leg and was pleased with how well it was healing. On one visit, he entered the house with a suit draped over his arm. "These pants and the jacket have rips in the seams. Can you fix em? Guess I ought a take the advice I give my patients and stop eating so darn much." After his examination of Emma, he lit a cigarette, donned his hat, and strode out the door with a wave.

The news from Europe sounded more ominous every day. Hitler's appetite for power was growing and it appeared no one could stop him. Mike and Laura silently wondered how long the United States could stay neutral and away from trouble.

Anna ran downstairs. "Mom!"

"In here, dear."

"There you are. Ned just called and wants to take me to the movies to see *The Adventures of Robin Hood*. Errol Flynn's in it and we'd like to take Lou with us 'cause I'm sure he'd like it. Okay?"

"It's fine with me as long as he has his homework done. By the way, I like Errol Flynn, too. Do you want to take me?"

"Another time, Mom. I can't have you going bananas over Errol Flynn while I'm sitting there with Ned."

Anna found Lou and said, "Hey, Louie, I have a question for you."

"Yeah, what is it?"

"How would you like to go to the movies with me and Ned tonight?"

"Huh? Sit in a dark room while you two get all kissy kissy? Yuk!"

"Suit yourself. We just thought you might like to see *The Adventures of Robin Hood*. Plus the serial this week is *The Lone Ranger*. Okay, see ya later."

"Hold on! You didn't tell me it would be *that* movie. Of course, I wanna go."

"Homework done?"

"Mostly. Let's go."

Lou was in seventh heaven watching the Lone Ranger, battle the bad guys without ever revealing his identity. *I want to be like him,* he thought. Then he sat back and munched popcorn while his other hero, Robin Hood, got the better of Prince John. Lou was enthralled for two hours as good fought evil again and again and won.

Ned watched the Movietone News with growing alarm as the problems in Europe lit up the screen. Watching the evil over there, he felt helpless and inadequate being nothing more than a Yale student in a safe country.

Chapter Twenty-Five

In December, Ned and Anna walked home from the movie theater, keeping their coats closed with one gloved hand and pulling their hats down with the other. The full moon lit up the sparkles in the snow beside the road. "It must be below freezing," said Anna as she shivered in the cold.

"Let's get you home where you can warm up," said Ned, "but make sure you don't tell Emma our secret."

"Oh, I won't. She'll be so surprised. I love you for doing this."

Ned stopped and looked at Anna with a serious expression on his face. "Do you really? Love me, I mean? Because I know I love you."

Now Anna stopped and gazed into Ned's face. Suddenly she was on a tropical island with warm sun, white beaches, and palm trees swaying. Birds were singing and waves gently lapped at the shore. Then she felt a snowy gloved hand on her cheek as Ned stood there, caressing her face. "Oh Ned," she finally managed to say, "I love you, too!"

They kissed and a car skidded around them; the driver honked his horn in anger.

Ned laughed. "He must not be in love."

They ran and skipped the rest of the way home. The two entered the door to the mud room and brushed the snow off themselves. Emma greeted them as they removed their coats and boots. "You two certainly look happy. Was the movie that good?"

Anna gave her sister a questioning look. "Movie? Oh right, the movie. It was okay."

Emma crossed her arms over her chest. "Okay then, what has you two grinning like a couple of jack o' lanterns? Hmm?"

Ned and Anna looked at each other and blurted out, "We're in love!"

Emma grabbed Anna's hand. "Sorry Ned, but you have to go home 'cause Annie and I have a lot to talk about."

Ned laughed and reached for his coat. "Okay, but you won't be so eager to get rid of me one day soon."

Emma shook her head. "I never know what the devil you're talking about."

Alone in their room, the twins sat on Emma's bed, talking and giggling until midnight. Lou could hear them through the wall, but he was too wrapped up in his own problems to pay much attention to them.

Christmas was drawing close and Lou wanted to do something special for his family. Money was tight and he didn't know what to get them even if he did have money.

The next day after school he talked to Gus about his problem. Gus listened to what he had to say and together they came up with a plan. For the next two weeks, Lou worked more on his gifts than he did on repairing cars, all with Gus's approval.

In the meantime, Anna and Ned had a surprise of their own. The two of them approached Emma one night as she sat on the sofa hemming a dress. Anna said, "Emmie, we've been thinking— "

"Oh oh, that can't be good," laughed Emma.

"Hush, just listen to us. Now, as I was saying, we've been thinking that you're wasting your beautiful looks sitting home all the time. You need to be out, having fun and enjoying life."

"That's right," chimed in Ned. "I think that if we worked on you a bit, you'd be presentable for society."

Anna punched him in the side. "Don't listen to him. But, you will thank him in a minute."

Emma's curiosity was aroused. "Okay, what do you two have planned that apparently includes me?"

Ned and Anna looked conspiratorially at each other, then Ned said, "I have a friend—"

"Oh God," cried Emma, "what is he, the bottom of Yale's barrel? Or does he even go to Yale? Is he your milkman?"

Anna put her fingers to her sister's lips to stop her from talking. "Just listen, Emmie."

Ned continued, "Like I said, I have a friend, at Yale, who's near the top of his class, good looking, wouldn't you say so Anna?"

"Definitely."

"And he's smart, but—"

"I knew it, there's a but."

"But," Ned went on calmly, "he's fairly new in town and doesn't know many people. Plus, he's shy so it's hard for him to meet girls."

"Why are you telling me this?"

"Because, we've shown him your picture and he's very interested in meeting you. Did I mention he was very interested?"

Now Emma sat up straight so she could pay more attention. "What's his name?"

Ned laughed. "Aha, now look who's interested. His name is Joe. Joseph Alan Montgomery. Tall, dark and handsome, all that stuff you girls say you like."

"Really? And he's interested in me?"

"Yes, Emmie," said Anna, "he wants to meet you. We thought we could all go to the movies tomorrow night on a double date. Now that your leg is nearly all healed and you can walk without a cane, we think it's the perfect time for you two to meet. What d'ya say?"

Emma stared at Ned. "There's one problem, he's seen my picture, but I haven't seen his."

"Not a problem little lady, here ya go." Ned produced a photograph of Joe and handed it to her.

Emma studied the picture. "You may call Mr. Montgomery and tell him Miss Emma Lee Dyson would like to make his acquaintance." Laughter from the three young people flowed into the kitchen where Laura and

Mike were listening to the entire conversation and grasping each other's hands in joy.

Christmas morning arrived while the Dysons were asleep. First Lou awoke, then Mike and Laura, and finally the girls. They all ended up in the living room, wearing pajamas, slippers and robes, a cup of hot cocoa in hand. Once the cover was pulled off the cage, Hope started the festivities with a lilting song.

The Christmas tree was small, but laden with handmade ornaments that the children had made since they were old enough to use scissors. Each one brought an exclamation of, "Remember when . . .?"

Under the tree sat a few wrapped gifts, each one bearing a name tag of one of the Dysons. Two of the gifts, a larger one and a small one, had Gus's name on the tag.

"Well, Lou," said Laura, "would you like to be Santa this year and pass out the gifts?"

Lou grinned. "Yes, ma'am, I would."

Lou crawled under the tree and started pulling out the gifts and handing them to their rightful owners, keeping the ones for himself on the floor near him. When all the gifts were disbursed, they started opening them. Shrieks of delight followed as one by one each person cradled a gift close to them and said, "It's exactly what I wanted!" Emma had knit hats and scarves for each person and Anna had written a poem for each member of her family. Without much money, Mike and Laura had managed to buy a birthstone ring for each of the girls and a wallet for Lou with a crisp, new, one dollar bill inside. For each other, Mike and Laura had all they could ever want sitting right there in the room with them.

Lou handed out one final gift to each, the one from him. Gus had shown him how to take black wire clothes hangers and cut, bend and weld them into various shapes five inches tall. Mike's was of a man sitting in one of Lou's small metal cars. Laura's was in the shape of a woman standing over a table, rolling pin in hand. Emma's was a young woman sitting in a chair sewing, and Anna's was a young woman standing in front of a filing cabinet. Lou saw the pleased look on each face. The gifts weren't store-bought, but he guessed they would do.

His gift to Gus was in the shape of an older man holding a wrench. Laura's gift to Gus was a box of home-baked goodies for him and his boys.

That afternoon, Ned and Joe stopped over to see the girls and to give them each a gift. Joe and Emma had been dating ever since the double date and were seldom apart, especially since Yale was closed for the holiday. *I wouldn't mind,* thought Emma, *to have this go on forever.*

Chapter Twenty-Six

January 5, 1939. Laura set a plate of eggs in front of Mike. "More toast?"

"No, thanks. I'm gonna eat what I've got, take a quick look at the paper, then head over to the office." Mike finished his eggs, then took his coffee cup in one hand and the newspaper in the other.

"Anything interesting?" asked Laura, blowing on her coffee.

"Not really. The United States has finally declared that Amelia Earhart is dead. I guess that after two years they figure that if she were still alive they'd have found some trace of her by now."

"What a shame. I always hoped she'd appear on a desert island one day, living like a native, but alive and well. Poor thing."

Mike turned the page. "Oh, here's something you might be interested in, but I probably shouldn't tell you. It's not that important." He grinned at Laura.

Laura jumped up and tried to read the paper over Mike's shoulder, but he kept moving the paper away from her. She finally grabbed it from him, a satisfied look on her face until she realized Mike let her take it. She read quickly through the articles, then let out a shriek.

"I see you found it," said Mike.

"Yes! The World's Fair is coming to New York! Can we go, huh, can we? Oh, the kids will love it."

"The kids? Really?"

"Okay, I'll love it. It'll be like 1904 all over again, except this time I'll be tall enough to see and old enough to remember the experience. What do ya think? Can we go?"

Mike stood and hugged his wife. "How can I say no to you. It's going to run from April to October this year and next so we ought to be able to make it one of those —"

Mike couldn't finish because Laura had her lips pressed against his in a passionate kiss. Lou walked in on the scene and started to back out on seeing his parents embarrassingly busy.

"Come here," said Laura, "we've got wonderful news to tell you. Get your sisters down here and we'll tell you all together."

Soon the twins and Lou were sitting at the table waiting to hear what had made their mother so happy. "I bet she's pregnant," whispered Emma.

"Eww, no!" said Anna. "Maybe she just inherited a fortune from a long lost rich uncle."

Lou sipped his juice. "Why don't we just ask her? So, Mom, what did ya wanna tell us?"

Laura sat down. "Do you remember me telling you about the '04 World's Fair?"

Anna sighed, "Yeah, about a hundred times, plus every time we have an ice cream cone."

Lou took another sip. "You planning to make us ice cream for breakfast?"

"No, silly," said Laura. "Your father and I are planning to take you kids to the World's Fair in New York City! What d'ya think about that?"

Emma jumped up so fast her juice spilled. Wiping it up, she said, "Really? We get to go not only to a World's Fair, but to New York City?"

"That's right."

"Did you hear that Annie? We're going to New York!"

"I heard! Dad, do you think Ned and Joe can go with us? If they want to, that is."

Mike ran a napkin across his face. "As long as they pay their own way, we can certainly let them ride with us."

"Yay!" shouted the girls. "Let's go see what we'll wear."

"Hold on," said Laura. "The Fair doesn't start until April and it runs for two years. I don't know when we'll go, but it'll be sometime this year, or next." Laura gave Mike a pleading look "Perhaps this summer when school is out?"

Mike straightened his tie, stood, and pushed his chair in. "If we can sell a couple of cars between now and then, sure. We can take a train into the city and have a good time. So, Anna, you'd better start hustling and get some cars sold if you want to go this year." Mike blew them a kiss and left for work.

Anna brightened. "I've got an idea for a sales ad that just might bring in more business. After breakfast, I'm gonna run it by Dad to see what he thinks. New York here we come!"

Emma glowed with the thought. "What's going to be there this year, does the paper say?"

Laura glanced through the paper again. "It's called the Dawn of a New Day and they say we'll get to see the world of tomorrow. Lemme see, oh here ya go, the Fair opens April 30th to coincide with the 150th anniversary of George Washington's Presidential Inauguration in New York City. Well now, isn't that something?"

"Boring," moaned Lou. "I sure hope they come up with something more interesting than that or ice cream cones."

While Laura and the girls dreamed about the Fair, Lou headed out the door to go to school. It was Thursday, the third day of school since New Year's and the temperature was a freezing fifteen degrees. As he pulled his hat down over his ears to keep the cold out, he stayed warm thinking about New York City in the summer.

Chapter Twenty-Seven

Friday July 14, 1939. Two days after Lou's sixteenth birthday, Mike, Laura, and Lou drove in one car while Ned, Anna, Joe, and Emma drove in another to the New Haven Railroad station. They parked near the station then entered to purchase train tickets. Posters of the World's Fair adorned the interior walls with a notice that the New Haven Railroad could get you there quickly and easily. Along with the tickets, the Dysons were each handed a brochure describing the Fair and a few of the many attractions the Fair offered.

Laura and Mike found a place on a well-worn waiting room bench. The younger generation found it impossible to sit still. Instead, they darted around the hot, musty, crowded room reading the train schedules and colorful posters and looking out the dirty windows every two minutes to see if the train was coming. When the station manager announced the train would arrive soon, everyone filed out onto the platform. Lou jumped when he heard a loud whistle, then a huge smile spread across his face as the train came into view.

Once settled on red velvet seats for the two-hour trip to New York, the passengers' eyes were fixed on the scenery passing by the windows. The train stopped every few minutes to pick up more riders until the coach was full. Excited passengers spent the trip reading the Fair guide, engaging in cheerful conversations amid a blue layer of cigarette smoke, and staring out the windows. As they rode on, they passed various views— backyards with clotheslines displaying sheets and all manner of personal apparel, empty neglected lots full of weeds and trash, and cities with taller buildings than could ever be found in New Haven. Finally, the train rumbled underground into a dark tunnel lit only by bare bulbs.

When the train stopped, the conductor grandly announced, "Grand Central Station, gather your things and enjoy your stay in New York." Everyone stepped off the train and walked alongside the tracks until they entered the cavernous Grand Central Station. The huge clock in the center of the room struck ten. Mike and Laura gathered the five children together, afraid of losing them in the middle of the chaos. At the information booth, Mike asked the attendant how to get to the Fair and was told to look for a blue and orange bus, the official colors of the Fair. The first bus they came to was full as were the second and third buses. Laura said, "Grand Central Station may be as close as we get to the Fair." A fourth bus pulled up and the Dyson party hopped on.

The ride from Manhattan to Flushing Meadows in Queens was a thrilling experience in itself. The buildings were so tall the passengers couldn't see the tops of them from the bus windows. "Look, Dad, the new Empire State Building!" Lou shouted as they drove by what was now the tallest building in the world. Pedestrians were everywhere, more people than they'd ever seen at one time. The closer they got to Queens, the more normal sized the buildings became. In no time, the bus pulled into a lot and parked in a spot next to a long line of similar buses. They had arrived at the World's Fair!

As excited as she was, Laura wondered if she and Mike would be able to keep the family together and not end up losing someone in the horde of people surrounding them.

Chapter Twenty-Eight

The air was hot with little breeze to cool them, but the excitement level was so high the heat was of minor consequence. With tickets and guides firmly in hand, Mike and Laura drew the children around them just inside the gate. Mike raised his voice to get them to focus on him instead of the myriad sights in front of them. "Everyone," he shouted, "listen to me. It's going to be nearly impossible to stay together all day, especially when we each have our own things we want to see and do." Mike looked at his watch. "It's 10:45; I suggest we meet somewhere at five o'clock." Mike searched the area around him. "See that huge round structure over there with the statue of George Washington in front?"

"Yeah."

"We'll all meet there at five, then go have dinner together. You got that?"

"Yes, sir," said Ned and Joe in unison.

Anne and Emma nodded.

Laura waited for Lou to respond, then saw that he was engrossed in the guide, mentally planning what he wanted to see. "Lou! What time are we to meet?"

'Huh? I don't know."

"Five o'clock. Where are we meeting?" she asked in frustration.

Lou grinned. "Over there by that large round thing. The guide calls it a Perisphere and the spikey thing next to it is a Trylon."

"Right, by George Washington. Five o'clock. Girls, be careful and hold your pocketbooks tight; we're in the city."

"Mom!" complained Emma. "We're nineteen, almost adults. We'll be careful, plus we've got the guys here to take care of us."

Mike looked squarely at Ned and Joe. "I'm trusting my girls to your care, boys. Nothing, and I mean nothing, better happen to them."

"Yes, sir."

After a round of hugs, as though they would never see each other again, the twins and their boyfriends went off in one direction, while Lou went in another. Mike and Laura headed for the Perisphere, eager to go up in it and see the utopian city of the future. Laura said, "I can't imagine how there could be anything else to invent. I mean, we have so many modern conveniences now, who could dream up anything more?"

"One thing I want to see," said Mike, "is the General Motors exhibit. This guide says it's a vision of what the future world of 1960 will look like. Don't know what more they can do with cars—four wheels, a motor, and a steering wheel is about all you need."

Laura forced a smile on her face that Mike noticed. "What's the matter? I thought you'd be in seventh heaven by now."

117

"I'm probably just being silly, but I'm worried about Lou being off by himself. At the '04 Fair I didn't have to watch out for anyone, I was the one being taken care of. Now we have five minors to get safely home."

"He'll be fine, sweetheart. They all will. Relax and enjoy the Fair. I have a feeling this is a day we'll never forget."

Ned saw something that made his heart race. "Look at that, Joe, a parachute jump! Wanna do it?"

Joe saw where Ned was pointing and consulted his guide. "Wow! This thing is 250 feet high and you get strapped to a real parachute. There are two seats to each chute so we can ride together. You bet I wanna do it!" Then looking at Emma, he asked, "Do you girls wanna go with us?"

The twins looked at each other, shuddered, and shook their heads.

"Are you okay if we go up in it?" asked Joe.

Emma smiled at the excited look on Joe's face. "We'll be fine, you go ahead. There's plenty to do down here, right Annie?" Anna nodded and gave Ned's arm a quick squeeze.

"It takes a minute to go up," said Joe, "and another twenty seconds or so to come down, so we won't be long." As they hurried to buy tickets and get in line, Anna heard Ned tell Joe that it was the way the Army trains its parachute jumpers.

Lou wandered around the grounds, checked his guide and marveled at the sights before him. He entered the Westinghouse exhibit, packed with people. As he was pushed through the crowd, he heard someone say, "My. . . brain . . . is . . . bigger . . . than . . . yours."

Lou stopped short and looked around to see who would have the nerve to say such a thing, then he looked up at a platform above him and saw the most amazing sight he'd ever seen—a large golden man made of steel. Lou was mesmerized. The middle-aged man standing next to the behemoth held a microphone and explained that the people were looking at Elektro, the moto-man and his dog, Sparko. "Elektro has a seven-hundred-word vocabulary; he can walk, talk, and even count." The audience gasped in unison.

The promoter said to Elektro, "How tall are you?"

Elektro said, "I . . . am . . . seven . . . feet . . . tall."

"That's right. Come here, Elektro."

The robot took one halting step, then another, until he was in front of the promoter.

There was another gasp from the onlookers.

"Now," said the promoter, "watch carefully at what Elektro will do next." The promoter took a cigarette out of a package, put it in the robot's mouth, and lit it with a match. Soon smoke appeared to be exhaled from Elektro's mouth. One woman fainted.

"Is there a doctor in the crowd?" someone yelled.

Lou knew there were a lot of exhibits he wanted to see, but he couldn't pull himself away from Elektro.

When at last he'd seen everything the robot could do, he made his way outside and found himself standing next to a large round post. On reading the inscription, he learned that right at that spot, fifty feet under the ground, was a time capsule. He'd heard of such things in school.

This time capsule, it said, was a tube containing current items of the day. In it were writings by Albert Einstein and Thomas Mann, copies of *Life Magazine*, a Mickey Mouse watch, a Gillette safety razor, a dollar in change, a pack of Camel cigarettes, seeds of foods like wheat, corn, oats, tobacco, rice, and such, and many more items to show how the people of 1939 lived. The inscription went on to say that the capsule could not be opened until the year 6939, five thousand years into the future. Lou read that again to make sure he read it right. Yup, it said 6939. Lou walked off, shaking his head and wondering what the world would possibly look like in five thousand years. Maybe all the people would look like Elektro.

Mike and Laura entered the RCA Pavilion and found a seat near the front where a strange object was on display. People were milling around, talking excitedly, and trying to touch the thing. Soon David Sarnoff, president of RCA, strode to the front of the room, cleared his throat, and began to speak. The room was silent as everyone waited to hear about this object.

"Ladies and Gentlemen," he began, "what you see before you is what we call a television." Oohs and ahhs could be heard throughout the room. "Watch closely as

I turn it on." Mr. Sarnoff turned a knob and before long a fuzzy image appeared on the screen. Some people nearest to the thing jumped back when a man could be seen sitting at a desk and talking to them.

"Well for goodness sakes," cried Laura. "That's President Roosevelt!"

"Yes, it is," said Mr. Sarnoff. "And believe it or not, he's at his desk in Washington, yet we can see and hear him right here in New York City."

The noise in the crowded room escalated as some people cheered and others scoffed, assuming it was a trick.

Mr. Sarnoff asked for quiet and explained, "His image is going through wires, from Washington, DC right to here. It's a whole new technology, like radio only with pictures. To prove to you it's not a trick, we have a television in the next room that has a transparent case so you can see the internal components for yourself. As an added treat, you can walk by and see yourselves on television. This way, please."

Mike and Laura quickly rose and followed him to the adjoining room where, along with the rest of the crowd, they filed in front of a camera and whooped with joy when they saw themselves on the tiny screen. "Now I've seen everything," laughed Laura. "Wait till we tell the kids about this!"

From the RCA building, they made their way over to the Chrysler building and entered an auditorium that was many degrees cooler than outside. A big sign on the stage announced that they were sitting in a room with a new invention called air conditioning. Laura leaned over to Mike and whispered, "I may never leave this room."

After watching a film on how a Plymouth is assembled, Mike whispered, "I may never leave this room, either. I'd like to see that film again."

When they finally forced themselves to exit into the heat, Mike looked at his watch and said, "We still have an hour to explore, then we'd better start heading toward George Washington."

A while later, Ned snapped open his pocket watch and announced, "It's nearly five; we'd better get over to the meeting point. No way do I want your parents to get upset with us."

As the four of them approached the statue, they saw Mike up ahead and called to him.

"Ah, here you are," said Mike. "Look, hon, right on time."

"Wonderful," said Laura, "have you seen Lou anywhere?"

Anna shook her head. "We haven't seen him all day."

Mike felt Laura squeeze his hand. "Don't go getting all worried, honey; he's still got five minutes. We'll wait right here for him."

Five minutes turned into ten and then fifteen. There was no sign of Lou anywhere.

Chapter Twenty-Nine

Lou meandered around the Fair, inhaling the aromas from the various food vendors and listening to the happy shrieks and laughter from the people around him. His destination was the Fun Zone because according to the guide, all the exciting rides were located there.

Lou looked up from the guide in time to see the parachute jump towering over him. He heard girls scream as they floated down to earth under a billowing canvas parachute. *I have to try that!* Lou paid his forty cents, got in line, and was soon settled in one of the double seats. A tall bare-chested man strapped himself into the seat next to him. Lou turned away, trying not to stare at him.

The seats started to rise and Lou felt his stomach drop as his body adjusted to the new sensation. Up, up they went on their way to the top, higher than Lou had ever been in his life. He found the courage to look down and was surprised at the tiny world below him. Lou turned to the man next to him to comment on the scene that was getting smaller by the second, but when he saw the man's face, he couldn't utter a sound. Finding his voice, he finally said, "You're . . . you're . . . Tarzan!"

The man smiled and nodded. "Yeah, that's me. Actually, my name's Johnny Weissmuller, but I'm sure you know me better as Tarzan."

"My name is Lou, may I shake your hand, sir?"

"Certainly. When we get back down, I'll find a pencil and sign your guide for you. If you want me to, that is."

"That would be swell! What are ya doing here at the Fair?"

"Having fun, like you, but actually, I'm in the Aquacade."

"Aquacade? What's that?"

"It's a water show with synchronized swimming and diving. There's lights and music, and—"

"You swim?"

Weissmuller grinned. "I guess you could say that. I've won five Olympic gold medals for swimming."

"For real? You mean I'm sitting next to a movie star and an Olympic gold medal winner? No one's gonna believe me."

"They will when I sign your guide for you. Do you swim, Lou?"

"Yeah, I've taken lifeguard lessons."

"Well, good for you. Lifeguards are important. They save people, just like Tarzan does, except he's fake and you're real."

Lou basked in the warm feeling enveloping him.

The ride stopped and Lou felt a jolt. "Here we go, back down to earth," his friend said as they found themselves drifting peacefully toward earth.

When they were unstrapped from their seats, Weissmuller kept his promise by borrowing a pencil from a staff member and signing Lou's fair guide. He signed it, *To my friend, Lou, from Johnny Weissmuller and Tarzan.* "Say Lou, my show starts in a few minutes. How 'bout I let you in and give you a front row seat. Would you like that?"

"Would I! That'd be swell!"

Lou walked past the clock that said 4:30, but never saw it; his eyes were fixed on Tarzan.

Chapter Thirty

Laura paced back and forth until the grass was flattened in front of George Washington. She stubbed out one cigarette after another. Checking her watch, she let out a sigh and continued pacing. "I knew it, I just knew it," she repeated. "I knew we shouldn't have let him go off by himself. I just know something's happened to him."

Mike took her arm to make her stand still. "Stop it, Laura, he's a big boy. He knows enough to check the guide and see where aid stations are. He probably got caught up in the Fair and isn't paying attention to the time."

"You think so?"

"Sure. While we're worrying about him, he's probably having a grand time."

"Well I'm not going to just sit here and wait. Stay here, I'll be right back."

With that, Laura stubbed out another cigarette and marched to the nearby RCA Pavilion muttering, "Why have modern technology if you can't put it to good use?" On entering, she saw David Sarnoff talking with an older man. "Excuse me," she said, interrupting their conversation, "but I need to ask you something."

Mr. Sarnoff turned and scowled at her impertinence, but softened when he saw the worried look on her face. "Yes ma'am, what can I do for you?"

Laura took a deep breath and said, "When my husband and I were here earlier, we were able to see ourselves on what you call television. Can we also talk to it and be heard?"

"Well, yes. What do you have in mind?"

"My sixteen-year-old son is missing and I wonder if I could describe him on your television so other people who come in here can see it and look for him."

Mr. Sarnoff put his hand on her shoulder. "I think that would be an interesting experiment for us to try. Come with me." He led her to a back room where a camera was set up. "Now, you look at this camera and tell us about him and the people out front will see you. If you come and do this every fifteen minutes for the next hour, a lot of people will see your plea. Will that be okay?"

Laura allowed her shoulders to relax as a tear glistened in the corner of her eye. She followed Mr. Sarnoff's instructions and told the camera about her son, that his name was Lou, he was sixteen and wearing overalls and a blue shirt. And he wore glasses. "If you find him," she said, "please have him meet his family at the George Washington statue."

She thanked him profusely and ran back to Mike and the kids, telling them what she just did.

Anna hugged her. "Mom, you're like a movie star!"

Laura lit a cigarette. "No, I just want to know Lou is safe."

Lou settled in a front row seat to watch the water show. He saw a line of women lean into the pool, one after another in unison, then make designs like a kaleidoscope while they swam. He enjoyed the clowns and the high divers and all the music and colored lights, but he was waiting for his hero.

Soon he saw men lined up on the rim of the pool; Tarzan stood in the middle, taller than the rest. When a whistle blew, they dove in and swam the length of the pool. Lou couldn't contain his excitement. He clapped and whistled as he watched his friend outswim all the rest. At the other side, the swimmers turned and swam back. Weissmuller emerged as the clear winner jumping out of the pool and waving at the crowd. He then looked over at Lou and gave him a two-finger salute.

Lou could only imagine what it must be like to swim and dive like the performers he'd just seen. They seemed so totally in control of their bodies. At the end of the show, Johnny Weissmuller walked past photographers and came over to Lou. "You having fun, son?" he asked with a wide grin on his face.

Lou could only nod his head. He'd never been happier in his life.

A thought suddenly took hold of Lou and his happiness vanished into the steamy, humid air. *I'm supposed to meet my family somewhere. What time is it? Is it five o'clock yet?* On his way out of the Aquacade, he was pushed and jolted and carried along with the crowd. Seeing a man with a watch, he stopped him and asked for the time.

"Five minutes ta six," the man said and hurried on.

Because he had followed Weissmuller into the show, Lou wasn't sure which way to go. Walking past the parachutes, he relaxed a little on seeing the familiar sight. Then he heard his name being called and turned to look, but didn't see anyone he knew. A woman approached him and said, "Are you Lou?"

"Yes."

"I'm glad you're safe. Your family is looking for you. You're to meet them by George Washington."

"Uh, thanks. Where—"

"That way," she said, pointing in the direction he needed to go. "Better hurry, your mother's worried sick."

Lou took off on a dead run.

Chapter Thirty-One

Mike held a chair for Laura in the Schaefer Food Center. When Lou had returned to them, Laura had been both too happy and too upset to be able to speak coherently so she elected to say nothing.

With menus in front of them, Lou felt the heaviness in the air and took his mother's lead by keeping quiet. Once again, he had proven he was a loser. Larry would have been back on time and wouldn't have made his parents worry. For the umpteenth time, he wondered why his parents were saddled with Screw-up Lou instead of Perfect Larry.

The waiter brought them seven hamburgers with fries, one bottle of beer and six bottles of Coca Cola. They ate in relative silence. Finally, with anxieties relieved and stomachs full, Mike turned his attention to Lou. In an effort to stifle his anger, he asked, "So, where were you?"

Lou looked at his plate with nothing but a pickle slice left on it. He hated pickles, but felt he ought to eat it as penance for what he'd done. Plus, it bought him a few more seconds before speaking. "I'm sorry," he said to the table. "I didn't mean to be late," he looked up and grinned, "but something wonderful happened."

The twins perked up and gave him their full attention. Mike said, "I'm still waiting."

Lou looked over at Ned and Joe. "Did you see the parachute jump?" he asked.

Emma rolled her eyes. "Did they see it? They went on it five times!"

"Well, I went on it once and the man sitting next to me was . . .."

"Was what?" Laura barked, her voice coming out sharper than she intended.

Lou let a smile out. "Not what, who."

"Okay, who?"

"None other than Johnny Weissmuller! You know, Tarzan!"

Ned and Joe gasped. "*The* Johnny Weissmuller? You sat next to him?"

Now Lou grinned. "I did and we talked and he autographed my guide, see right here" he held it up for them to see, "and then he let me into the Aquacade because he's in it because he's won five gold medals for swimming in the Olympics. He let me sit in the front row for free."

"Wow!" said Mike. "I guess you did have an adventure. But," he looked over at Laura, "you should have kept a better eye on the time. Your mother was worried."

"I know. I'm sorry. Who was that woman who found me?"

Laura looked at Mike and smiled for the first time since five o'clock. "It worked, Mike, it worked! Television can actually be useful."

On the train ride home, everyone in the coach was animated and excited, eager to share their fun experiences at the Fair.

"Dad," said Anna, "they have electric typewriters now. Can you believe it? We should get one for the office as soon as they're available."

"Mom," squealed Emma, "did you see the nylons? We don't have to wear wool or silk stockings anymore. Nylons are prettier and stronger. I just have to get me a pair!"

Lou stared at his autographed guide, bursting with excitement and looking forward to sharing his good news with Gus.

Laura nodded and fought to keep her eyes open. "I really hope that with all that's going on over in Europe, this World's Fair will be able to bring peace and understanding to the world. I read that sixty countries were represented at the Fair. Maybe this will settle the unrest and we can all come together in peace." Laura fell asleep as the train rumbled on.

Chapter Thirty-Two

Saturday, June 21, 1941. The Dyson's backyard hummed with activity. Colored lights lit up the trees like fireflies and crepe paper decorated the porch. The picnic table groaned as more and more food appeared on its checkered tablecloth. Mike carried kitchen chairs outside and set up a small table to hold gifts. With a bit of crepe paper left over, Emma had added bows to the table. Laura carried out a tray of condiments, glasses, and napkins and set them on the picnic table.

Alice and Stuart Dyson relaxed in lawn chairs and chatted with Gus about how cars had improved since they were the owners of Dyson's Cadillacs. Alice nursed a glass of wine; Stuart enjoyed a bottle of beer. Gus held a cold soda bottle against his cheek to cool down from the heat.

"Can I help, Laura?" asked Mike's mother.

"I don't think so, Alice." "I believe we've got everything under control. You and Stuart must be tired from your long trip. How long did it take you to drive up from Florida?"

Alice sighed. "Four days! We spent three nights in tourist cottages along the way. I swear I was never so happy to see New Haven!"

"I can imagine. Are you still glad you moved south?"

"Heavens yes, we enjoy having no more icy winters to contend with. My hope, of course, is that one day you'll be able to come down and visit us."

Laura found a rock to hold down the napkins. "I expect we just might now that Lou is out of school."

Gus rose and went into the house and Alice called to Lou. "Lou, baby, come here." He walked over to his grandmother. "That was a nice graduation tonight, Lou. I was bursting with pride when you walked up to get your diploma. What do you plan to do now that you're out of school?"

"I'm not sure come fall, but for the summer, I plan to do as I do every year, work in the garage for Gus during the week and work as a lifeguard on the weekends."

"I'm so glad we turned the dealership over to your dad. What's it been, fifteen years now? My, he's done a fine job with it. Do you like working there?"

"Yeah, Gram, I do. I can just about take a motor apart and put it back together blindfolded. Gus has taught me an awful lot."

"Well isn't that something? I remember what a help Gus was to us, too." She lowered her voice. "I was so sorry to read the letter from your mother about Gus' poor wife. What a pity. Are his boys doing okay?"

"Yeah, Gram. Two of them are in their twenties, so he's only got thirteen-year-old Eric home with him. He says they help each other out."

Alice looked worried. "I read in the paper that Roosevelt reinstated the draft last year. Have you registered?"

"No, Gram, not yet. I don't turn eighteen until next month. But Ned and Joe both had to register last year."

"Oh dear. I hope they can stay in Yale and not have to go to war. I remember your dad leaving to go fight in the great war. I was scared to death he wouldn't come back home." Alice reached for Lou and patted his hand. "You stay safe dear, you hear?"

"Yes, Gram."

"Attention, everybody," called Laura. "The food's ready, come get a plate!"

Everyone crowded around the table ready to fill a paper plate and find a seat. The twins, along with Ned and Joe, found chairs under a tree; two of Lou's friends from high school sat on the picnic benches with Lou.

Stuart fixed a plate for Alice and brought it to her. "You okay, love? You look tired."

"I'm okay. But I'd be lying if I said I wasn't looking forward to that guest bed tonight."

Laura tapped her glass with a spoon to get everyone's attention. "Raise your glasses, folks. I propose a toast to my son, Louis Dyson, a Class of '41 high school graduate. Here, here!" Glasses clinked and people clapped and yelled 'speech.'

Lou's face turned red as he stood and faced his family and friends. He made a quick bow and said,

135

"Thank you, thank you. You're very kind, but I didn't do anything. All I did was stay in school, thanks to my friend, Gus." He winked at Gus. "But since we're here doing this, I'd like to give honor to my brother, Larry, who would have also graduated tonight." He raised his glass of cherry Kool-Aid high in the air.

The small gathering then reveled in Laura's three-tier chocolate cake covered with fresh strawberries, completely unaware that in six months the country would be turned on its end.

Chapter Thirty-Three

Lou climbed up to the top of the lifeguard platform, donned his hat and sunglasses, applied lip balm, wrapped his whistle around his neck, and began his shift. He placed the binoculars and first aid kit on the seat next to him, just in case. He slowly swiveled his head back and forth while his eyes constantly scanned the glistening blue water. *This is the life. And to think I get paid for doing this. I love working for Gus, but nothing beats being outside in the fresh salt air.*

It was a late July afternoon and the beach was dotted with blankets and umbrellas as far as Lou could see. Children played along the edge of the shore squealing at every pretty shell then scooped water into a plastic pail for making mud castles. Older children ventured further into the Sound where the waves came up to their waists. Beyond them, teenagers and adults ran and dived head first into the frothy surf, their feet sticking up in the air as they explored the muddy depths. It was nearly high tide; the waves splashed against the shore, only to recede and come back again and again determined to encroach on the sunbathers' territory.

Jerry, the lifeguard Lou was relieving, climbed halfway up the platform. "Keep an eye on that group over there," he pointed to his left. "Those teenagers on the red blanket think it's fun to run into the water, duck under the surface, then wave their hands like they're drowning. I've blown my whistle at 'em, but they keep doing it. Kids!"

Lou looked to his left. "Got it. Anything else I should be aware of?"

Jerry motioned to a blue umbrella. "Well, there's a dame in a yellow bathing suit under that umbrella who's a real dish. A gen-u-ine humdinger. You might wanna keep your eye on her."

"Get outta here. I think I can handle things while you go take a break. But really, the blue umbrella?"

Jerry whistled and climbed down, heading for the refreshment stand.

Lou settled into the rhythm of the beach, getting accustomed to the people's habits so he'd be better able to spot something out of the ordinary. A volleyball game was in progress at one side and further down the beach a man was being covered in sand by his children. A woman had set up an easel on the beach and was attempting to paint a seascape, whenever the offshore breezes would allow. It seemed to Lou she was engaged in a losing battle.

"Mister. Hey mister."

Lou looked down and saw a boy of about ten looking up at him. "Yes? What's the matter?"

"I cut my foot on a broken glass bottle. Can ya fix it?"

"You bet, I'll be right down." Lou grabbed the first aid kit and climbed down. He saw bloody footprints in the sand, ending where the boy stood. In no time, the wound was cleaned and bandaged and the boy was advised to watch where he walked.

The boy started to limp off, then turned and said, "Thanks mister," before running back to his mother.

Lou climbed back up the platform, happy to have been of service. Moments like that broke up the monotony, yet weren't a matter of life and death.

From somewhere to his right, a scream pierced the peaceful scene. His senses on high alert, Lou lifted his binoculars to search for the source of the sound. His eyes fell on arms waving in the water. He wondered if those were the kids Jerry had talked about, but he couldn't take a chance so he scurried down and ran as fast as he could into the water.

Just as the swimmer was about to go under again, Lou grabbed her, got her head above water, and brought her to shore. Lou laid the limp young lady, clad in a yellow bathing suit, on the sand, turned her on her side, and began resuscitation efforts. Salt water gushed from her mouth then the young woman began gagging and coughing, a sign that she'd be all right. He sat her up and supported her head with his strong hand. "You'll be okay now, ma'am. But if I were you, I'd stay close to shore if you can't swim."

The woman, who couldn't be much more than seventeen, started to stand, then fell back into Lou's arms, weak from the ordeal. "You saved my life. Thank you. My name's Karen, what's yours?"

Lou looked over at the blue umbrella, empty except for a blanket spread under it, then looked at the young lady in his arms and had to agree with Jerry, that oh yeah, she was a humdinger for sure. "I'm Lou," he said, suddenly unsure of what to do. His lifeguard training hadn't prepared him for something like this.

He saw Karen fixate on his wet chest hairs that glistened in the sun and wondered if she also noticed his muscles. Then he saw her motion toward the teenagers over on the red blanket. "I've been watching those jokesters horse around all day, pretending to drown, never thinking I'd be doing the same thing, except I wasn't pretending. I don't know how to repay you."

"No need, ma'am, I mean, Karen. Just doing my job. But if you'd like, I'm off duty in a couple of hours, I could treat you to a soda, if you'd like."

"I'd like that very much, Lou."

Chapter Thirty-Four

For the rest of the summer, Lou found himself whistling wherever he went and whatever he did. Whether he was taking apart a greasy motor or walking upstairs to his room, he whistled. But he especially whistled when his lifeguard shift began because he knew that if he was on the beach, Karen would be there, too. She brought her friends to meet Lou and always introduced him as the man who saved her life.

One day Anna and Emma took a trip to the Sound to investigate this lady of the beach who had their little brother wrapped around her sun-tanned finger. They were going to set her straight in no uncertain terms because nobody messed with their brother. As they took their sandals off and plodded through the wet sand, they found Karen sitting under her blue umbrella reading John Steinbeck's newest novel, *The Grapes of Wrath.*

Anna looked at her sister and raised her eyebrows in a questioning gesture. Maybe they'd been a little too quick to pass judgment. "Hello," said Anna, "I'm Anna and this is Emma, we're Lou's sisters."

"We're here," said Emma, "because we've wanted to meet you since the first day Lou started talking about you."

Karen put her book down and invited the twins to share her blanket. "It's nice to meet you; Lou mentions you two all the time. So, do I pass inspection?"

Emma stuttered. "What, ah—"

Karen laughed. "Don't worry, I have a kid brother, too. I know just how you feel."

The three of them relaxed and spent the rest of the day getting to know each other better.

That night at dinner, Emma kissed Lou on the head to his chagrin, and said, "You have our blessings to continue to see Karen. We approve of her."

Lou rubbed his head with a napkin to get the kiss off. "Gee, swell. Nice to know you approve, since I was gonna continue to see her anyway."

"Well," said Anna, "now that we've checked her out, we're wondering if you and Karen would like to go with us and our guys to Savin Rock Friday night."

"The amusement park?"

"Yeah. The six of us could have a blast on the roller coaster and in the arcade. What d'ya say, will you ask her?"

"Sure. Sounds like fun."

The three couples strolled from one attraction to another in the warm August evening. Shrieks came from the roller coaster on their left and the fun house on their right. They each had a hot dog in one hand and clung to their partner with their free hand. Music blared from one ride to another and hawkers called to them to try their skill at the games. "Five chances for a quarter! Come over and win a prize for your girl."

Ned stepped up, plopped down his quarter, and took the five darts handed to him. In front of him was a board covered with colored balloons. Ned put a dart in his right hand, brought his arm back, and let the dart fly. Pop! "One down, four to go," called the huckster. In swift order, Ned broke all five balloons, winning Anna a black and white panda bear which she hugged with all her might.

Not to be outdone, Joe threw rings at Coke bottles, scoring four out of five. Emma walked away with a kewpie doll.

Karen glanced at Lou, wondering what he would do to win her something. Lou walked resolutely over to the tower that had a bell on top and put down his quarter. Printed on the backboard were words like Wimp, Girl, Weak, Boy, Man and so forth, all the way up to Strongman. All he had to do was ring the bell once to win something. Lou had watched men try, lose, and walk away dejected. The hawkers were jeering, "Who's got a little muscle? Where are all the men? Don't be a sissy." Lou picked up the sledgehammer and said a quick prayer, then added to himself. *Don't let this be a time you screw up. For once in your life, Lou, do something right.*

Lou grabbed the hammer and raised it over his head. *This thing is heavier than I thought.* In one swift move, he made an arc and brought the hammer crashing down on the lever. The puck flew up past Atta Boy, past Wow! past Strongman, and made the bell clang. Lou dropped the hammer and shook life back into his shoulder while Karen threw her arms around his neck. She quickly picked out a stuffed dog that was almost as big as she was.

143

"His name is Louie," she announced proudly, "and I'm keeping him forever."

Part Two

Chapter Thirty-Five

Late August 1941. Lou received a letter saying Uncle Sam wanted him to register for selective service. Ned was at the house at the time and asked Lou if he wanted a ride to the draft board.

"Sure."

Lou hopped on the back of Ned's second-hand Indian Scout motorcycle. By the time they arrived at the draft board, Lou could care less that his hair was a mess; he only cared about the thrilling, powerful machine that had brought him into town. He impatiently waited in line to register, wanting the ordeal to be over so he could get back on the bike.

Arriving home, Mike put his arm around Lou and said, "I'm proud of you, son. It's uplifting to do something for your country, even if it's only registering for the draft. I remember how I felt; I just hope Roosevelt means it about not getting involved overseas."

"Me, too. Have you ridden on Ned's bike, Dad?"

"Yeah, once. But I prefer a solid car under me. Why, did you like it?"

"Dad, it was the keenest thing I've ever done. Ned wants me to help him work on the motor!"

"Well that ought to be right up your alley. Have fun. Here's something else that might interest you; I read in the paper today that when they dismantled the trylon and perisphere from the World's Fair, the whole forty million tons of steel went to the war effort."

"Good! Glad to see the steel's being put to good use. It sure gave us good memories."

Over the next few weeks, Lou spent every spare moment, when he wasn't with Karen, learning all he could about motorcycles and becoming Ned's number one mechanic. He got permission from Mike and Gus to add a sign to the garage reading, *We Fix Motorcycles.* Business increased as young men brought their bikes to them for repair. Test driving them afterwards was the highlight of Lou's day once Karen was back in school and he wasn't seeing her as often.

Chapter Thirty-Six

December 7, 1941. On Sunday morning, the family as usual attended their local church. The service was uneventful. The pastor, as was his custom, had prayed for the people in Europe and the bombings they were enduring on a daily basis. Just the thought of such atrocities made Laura shiver.

Back home, Laura changed into casual clothes, then busied herself decorating the rooms with Christmas garlands. Having changed into blue jeans, Mike turned on the living room radio to keep up with the news, then he and Lou grabbed a sandwich and settled onto the living room sofa to listen to the end of a football game. When the fourth quarter ended, their team had won twenty-one to seven. Father and son cheered and clapped until a breaking news announcement shattered their joy.

We interrupt this program to bring you a special news bulletin. At 7:55 am Hawaii time, Japanese dive bombers, fighter bombers and torpedo planes attacked the U.S. naval base at Pearl Harbor on Oahu. Approximately 360 Japanese planes took part in the attack which lasted less than two hours. More details are not available at this time. Stay tuned for more—attention, we have just heard from the White House that Japanese airplanes have also attacked Army and Navy bases in Manilla. It is expected that President Roosevelt will ask Congress to declare war on Japan and that Congress will approve his request.

"Laura!"

"Yes, Mike. I heard. Why is Japan bombing us? What does it mean?"

"I don't know, hon. Let's wait and see. But I don't like it. I don't like it at all. Girls, get down here!"

Hearing the urgency in their dad's voice, the twins stopped what they were doing and bolted downstairs to see what was going on. "What is it, Dad?"

"Japan has just bombed our ships in Hawaii, a United States territory. We may be getting into the war after all, like it or not."

The girls looked at each other in panic. No words were needed between them as they both knew the other's thoughts concerning their boyfriends.

From that moment on, all regular radio broadcasts were discontinued in an effort to keep listeners up to date on the news from Hawaii. On Monday, President Roosevelt made the sobering announcement that Congress had met and the United States had declared war on Japan. He said, "Yesterday, December 7, is a date which will live in infamy."

Three days later, while the country was still reeling from the Japanese attack, Hitler declared war on the United States. Now the country was fully involved in war on two continents.

Moments after the latest broadcast, Ned and Joe arrived at the Dyson's door. The mood in the house was subdued as talk of anything but the war seemed trivial. Prior conversations of clothes, movies, or meals, paled in importance to the United States' involvement in yet another world war.

Anna wrapped her arms around Ned. "I suppose you heard the news," she said.

"Yes, sweetheart, and Joe and I have something to tell you folks."

All chatter stopped as everyone focused their full attention on the two men.

Ned took Anna's hand and looked into her blue eyes while Joe did the same with Emma. Emma was shaking.

"Joe and I," said Ned, "plan to sign up for the Army Air Corps and go fight this war. This time," he allowed himself a slight smile, "we'll be using real parachutes and jumping from real planes."

Anna felt her body go limp. With a voice barely audible, she asked, "How soon?"

"Soon as possible. We plan to go down to see the recruiter this week. Right Joe?"

Joe looked at Emma and wiped the tears pooling in her eyes. "Right."

Emma's voice cracked. "But what about Yale? You two aren't ready to graduate yet."

"I know, Em, but we can finish our schooling later. I expect a lot of things are gonna be put on hold until the war is over."

Lou had been listening intently to the conversations, his mind racing with possibilities.

Chapter Thirty-Seven

Lou wiped his hands on a towel after fixing an electrical system in a customer's car, then sat next to Gus and picked up a cup of coffee. "What do you hear from Karl and Gus Jr? Did they get to Fort Jackson alright? South Carolina must be a whole new world compared to New Haven."

Gus took the towel and swiped at an oil spot on the work bench. "They called me when they got there, but I haven't heard much from 'em since. Guess the Army's keeping 'em busy with their basic training. Did Ned and Joe get to their base in North Carolina? Greensboro is it? Wouldn't want to jump out of no airplane. Would you?"

"Oh yeah, I think it would be fun, but I've got other ideas."

"Ya? Like what?"

"I haven't told Dad yet, but I'm thinking of joining the Navy."

"The Navy, huh?"

"Yup. I'd be going to the Great Lakes Training Center."

"After boot camp, what d'ya wanna do?"

Lou swept the garage with his arm. "Well, you've taught me so well here, Mr. Gus, that I want to learn how to repair airplanes. You know, be on a carrier and keep the planes running. What d'ya think?"

Gus broke into a big smile. "I think the Navy would be mighty lucky to have you and I'd be gosh awful proud of you."

Lou patted Gus on the knee. "Thanks, boss. Guess I'll go tell my folks. Wish me luck."

An hour later, Laura sat at the kitchen table crying. Her apron had gone from dry to damp with her tears. Mike stood behind her, his hands resting lightly on her shoulders. Lou paced around the kitchen, too excited to sit.

"Dad," said Lou, "you understand, don't you? I mean, you joined up to go fight in the great war."

"Yes, son, I do understand. And so does your mother; it's just going to take a little while for her to accept the fact that her baby is going off to war."

"Baby?"

Laura wiped her cheek. "Yes, Lou, you're my baby. Always were and always will be. Promise me you'll be careful."

"Mom! I'm eighteen and doing what Ned and Joe and Karl and Gus Jr. are doing. Dad, talk to her."

"Don't worry, son, she knows this is something you have to do. Just come home to her, like I did."

"I promise. I'm gonna go see the recruiter tomorrow."

Laura cried out. "Tomorrow?"

"Mom, it won't make it any easier if I wait a few more days."

Mike squeezed his wife's shoulders. "He's right, hon. The quicker we adjust to the idea, the better. Gus won't need him in the garage. Most of the young guys driving motorcycles have joined up, so that part of our business is about gone. To make matters worse, Cadillac is going to stop building cars and gear up to produce military equipment like the other car makers are doing. Roosevelt is calling it the Arsenal of Democracy. I sure hope this war ends soon, I don't know how we'll manage if it drags on."

Laura reached up and patted Mike's hand. "We made it through the Depression and we'll make it through this."

Anna, with Emma right behind her, came into the kitchen. "You got a stamp, Mom?"

"Another letter to Ned?"

"Yeah. Emmie and I try to write to our guys every day. And if they can't get mail during boot camp, we know they'll get 'em eventually."

Emma asked, "What's going on with you, Louie? You look like the cat that ate the canary." She glanced over at the yellow bird in its cage. "Sorry Hope, just an expression."

"I'm going to join the Navy," Lou answered. "I wanna fix the planes your guys will be flying."

"No kidding? You okay with that, Mom? Oops, I guess not. Sorry."

Lou stepped onto the bus and waved goodbye to his family that had come to see him off. To his surprise, Gus had joined them and sharply saluted him. Once he was seated and the bus started to move, Lou realized he'd never been away from home before. The thought of boot camp was as exciting as it was scary. He thought of Larry and wondered if he'd be proud of his screw-up brother. *I'm gonna make you proud of me, Larry, if it's the last thing I do.*

Chapter Thirty-Eight

"Mom!" Anna called out as she ran into the kitchen, a torn envelope in one hand and a letter in the other.

Laura set aside her checkbook and bank statement and gave full attention to her out-of-breath daughter. "Yes, sweetheart, what's up?"

"I got a letter from Ned! He finished basic training and he's on his way home! He'll be going to his parents' house first, of course, but then he'll come to see me."

"Wonderful. Is Joe coming home, too?"

"Yes! I've got a letter here for Emmy; gotta go." With that, Anna left the room as quickly as she'd entered it, leaving Laura feeling as though she'd just stepped into a whirlwind.

Two days later, Anna and Emma wore their best dresses, had their hair curled, and paced the living room. Laura walked in and said, "They won't get here any faster if you wear out the carpet. Here, take these dust rags and dust the furniture while you pace."

"Eww!" cried Emma, backing away. "We don't want to get our hands dirty before they get here!"

Laura laughed. "Any guy worth his salt wants to know his woman can clean a house. It won't kill you." With that, she handed them each a dust rag which they gingerly grasped with a thumb and one finger.

When the doorbell rang, two dust rags flew by Laura's head as the girls ran to open the door. The twins and their guys embraced for so long, Laura didn't think she'd get a chance to properly greet the two handsome men in their crisply-ironed uniforms. Laura called Mike to come home for a minute to say hello.

That night, Anna and Emma hung around the kitchen after the dishes were done, rather than run off to their rooms. They found small things to do as an excuse to dawdle until Laura finally said, "Okay, girls, out with it. What's going on?"

Emma cleared her throat, then again, and finally said, "We have something we want to talk to you and Dad about."

"Okay, let's go in the living room. Mike, can you shut the radio off for a few minutes?"

Laura sat next to Mike and looked from one twin to the other. "Alright, you have our attention, what's on your minds?"

The girls looked at each other, then at the floor, then burst into smiles. "Mom, Dad," began Anna, "Ned and Joe have asked us to marry them while they're home. They won't be home long 'cause they'll be leaving for flight school in Texas in a few days. A lot of their friends in the service planned to come home and get married and Ned and Joe want to marry us! Can you believe it? We'll have husbands in the Air Corps and have military benefits and I'll be Mrs. Ned Andrews—"

"And I'll be Mrs. Joe Montgomery!" chimed in Emma. "So, what do you say, is it okay with you? Do we have your blessings? Please?"

Laura looked at Mike, unable to speak for a few minutes. Then, after arranging her thoughts, she fought back the urge to yell or maybe laugh at her naïve girls and said in as calm a voice as she could muster, "Just because everybody else does something, doesn't make it right for you. Think back to the World's Fair, did you go on the Parachute Jump?"

"No."

"Why not?"

"I was scared."

"Did Joe ask you to go on it with him?"

"Yes."

"But you still said no, because you were afraid and weren't ready to take that step. If you had gone on, it would have been because he wanted you to, not because you felt it was right. Are you with me so far?"

The girls hung their heads. "Yeah."

Mike spoke up. "Do you love your guys?"

The girls looked up and beamed. "Yes!"

"Well, then," said Mike, "you'll do what's best for them. They're about to go to flight school where they need to concentrate, then they'll be sent into combat. Do you not think they'll have enough on their minds without worrying about you two?"

The girls stopped smiling.

156

"Do what your mother did and wait for them to come home when it's over. You'll have a much better idea at that time if marriage is what you still want."

Laura added, "If your love is real, and I expect it is, it will last until they get home. I know you're both twenty-one and don't need our permission to get married, but wouldn't you like to have a real wedding, not a hurried-up affair? Also, if you wait until the war is over, your brother will be home to celebrate the day with you. Wouldn't you like that?"

The girls looked at each other and slowly nodded.

Laura suggested they go to their room and mull over the advantages and disadvantages of having a rushed wedding.

The twins looked crestfallen as they left the room and headed upstairs.

Laura turned to Mike, "The poor things, we really burst their bubble, didn't we?"

Mike stubbed out his cigarette. "We wouldn't be doing our job if we didn't burst a few bubbles now and then. Let's see what they decide after they talk it over."

In their room, the girls each flopped on their own beds, their thoughts running rampant, clashing into and rolling over each other in their heads.

Emma finally sat up, wiped her eyes, and said, "Mom made sense, darn it."

Anna sat up. "I know, so did Dad. I guess they ought to know, they've both been where we are. But still—"

Emma grinned, "But still, I want to marry Joe!"

"And I want to marry Ned."

"Do you think Dad's right, that we'd be keeping their minds off their job and maybe putting them in harm's way?"

"I don't know. But I'd never want to do anything that would put Ned in danger."

"Nor would I. And what if, oh my gosh, I just thought of something."

"What, Em?"

"What if we were to get" she brought her voice to a whisper, "pregnant."

"Pregnant?" gasped Anna. "I hadn't thought of that. If that happened, we'd be raising our babies by ourselves and they might not know their daddies for years!"

"And," said Emma, "that's assuming our guys come home from the war safe and sound. I wonder if Mom is right, maybe we ought to wait."

"I don't like to admit it, but I'm beginning to agree with her. Should we go tell them?"

Emma nodded and they walked downstairs.

Mike and Laura looked up when the twins entered the room. They were happy to see that their girls looked less deflated than before.

Emma spoke for both of them, "We knew we could depend on you to steer us right. But," she laughed, "we were really looking forward to being married."

"I know," said Laura, "but I expect you were more enthralled with the idea of marriage than with actually getting married. You'll know when the time is right."

The next day when the boys came over, Anna and Emma told them they were honored, but would wait to marry them once the war was over. The girls noticed a slight relaxing of their boyfriends' shoulders.

Chapter Thirty-Nine

Lou stepped off the bus, weary, hungry, and rumpled. He had creases across his face from sleeping against his arm. His feelings alternated between being scared and being eager to see what the future had in store for him. He had met a few guys on the long bus trip and hoped he'd be put in the same barracks with them as they seemed friendly enough. As the new recruits were hurried across the field to the processing building, smartly-uniformed sailors on parade looked over at them and shouted, "You'll be sorreee!"

With no time to think, they were all ordered into a building where their papers were processed, then taken into a room lined with barber chairs. When it was Lou's turn, he sat in a chair, the barber turned him away from the mirror and covered him with a black cape. "You wanna keep your hair, recruit?"

"Yes, sir."

"Then hold out your hands and catch it."

Lou heard a buzzing sound as the shaver pressed against his forehead and glided down the back of his head. In less than two minutes his brown hair lay on the floor. He touched his head and felt nothing but stubble. With no time to mourn the loss of his hair, he was herded into another room where the men were told to strip. Lou did as he was told and entered a line with more bare men than he'd ever seen in his life. They came in all colors and sizes, some trying to cover themselves with their hands and others acting as though they went around undressed all the time. Lou never felt so exposed and his hands immediately crossed in front of him.

Before he could prepare himself for it, Lou smelled something antiseptic and cold and felt a jab in his upper arm. He rubbed the area and continued to follow the man ahead of him. Then he was weighed and measured, had his blood pressure taken and was given hearing, dental, and eye tests, including a new pair of glasses. He was poked, prodded and examined in places no person had ever gone before. Finally, he was given a small container and told to fill it. Returning with the filled container, he found himself shoved into another line where he was told to hold out his arms. As he walked down a line, Navy personnel piled on him shirts, pants, underwear, socks, toiletries, shoes, a small pocket New Testament, a sea bag, mattress cover, pillow, and blankets. Then he was shown into the barracks that would be his home for the next few weeks, He immediately got dressed, knowing his civilian clothes were being sent home to his parents. Lou looked around and was relieved to see that three of the men he'd met on the bus, Danny Epstein, Eric Carlson, and Red O'Reilly, had been assigned to his barracks.

Petty Officer Clarke entered the room, looking large and impressive. "Listen up, men," he said, "you're in the Navy now. You're not home with your mama, you're here with me and I ain't your mama. I don't ask you what you want to do, I tell you what you're going to do and you'd better do it fast and do it right. Got that?"

"Yes, Sir!" shouted the men.

"From now on it's aye, aye, sir! You got that?"

"Aye, aye sir!"

"You sleep on that bunk, you make it; you wear those uniforms, you wash 'em; you walk on that deck, you clean it. Do I make myself clear?"

"Aye, aye, sir."

"I can't hear you."

"Aye, aye, sir!"

The rest of the day went by in a blur as Lou followed the barking orders of Petty Officer Clarke. Before lights out, he was allowed a call home to say he had arrived and would contact his family by letter in two or three weeks. Nothing more.

Lou fell on his bunk, exhausted. He heard Taps playing somewhere and thought, *What have I gotten myself into?*

Chapter Forty

Lou sunned himself on the beach as waves gently lapped the shore. He heard a loud noise and a man shouting. Was someone drowning? A horn blared reveille and he quickly awoke and remembered where he was. He sat up quickly and bumped his head against Red's bunk above him. Looking around the room, he saw Petty Officer Clarke, in full uniform, banging a garbage can lid, and moving from bunk to bunk barking the men awake. It didn't take long for all eighty men to stand in disarray in front of their bunks, looking bleary-eyed and disheveled.

"You have five minutes to use the head, shave, dress, square your bunk and assemble outside!" yelled the Petty Officer as he stomped out the door.

The recruits scrambled over and around one another in an attempt to carry out his orders. Once outside, the cold January wind blowing off Lake Michigan was a bitter reminder that Lou wasn't on a beach in the middle of summer. The Petty Officer appeared more bothered by the slow-moving snails in his charge than by the weather.

"Move it, move it, move it!" he shouted.

Totally out of step, the recruits marched to the mess hall for breakfast. For the first time in Lou's life, hot coffee seemed like a luxurious treat. Wolfing down breakfast, Lou pictured his mom, dad and the twins sitting at the table, enjoying a relaxed breakfast and planning their day. His reverie was short-lived when he heard his name called. "Dyson, let's go." It was Red, now known as Recruit O'Reilly.

The rest of that day flew by in a blur as the recruits stood in line to learn military drill and the proper order for folding clothes and how to pack a sea bag, then lined up for physical training, lined up for mess hall, and lined up again to learn the details of rank and rating and what it means to be a member of the United States Navy. By the end of the day, Lou was tired and sore and more than ready to fall onto his bunk.

By the fifth day of boot camp, the raw recruits were awake, ready, and lined up outside in record time. They marched to the mess hall in step, feeling and looking more like a military unit than like the rag tag boys they were when they'd arrived just a few days ago.

The second week brought with it more marching and physical training. "Listen up," barked Petty Officer Clarke, "do you snails see that Rooster flag in front of those barracks?"

"Aye, aye, sir."

"I said do you see it?"

"Aye, aye, sir!"

"I want that flag in front of *our* barracks. Do you know how we get that flag in front of our barracks?"

"No sir!"

"We earn it! We earn it by marching better than any other company on this base. How do we get the Rooster flag?"

"We earn it, sir!"

"I want that flag flying on our barracks next week. How do we get it?"

"We earn it, sir!"

Marching drills took on a whole new meaning as Lou, Red, Danny, Eric and the others concentrated on getting the Rooster flag for Clarke. Disappointing him was not an option. By the end of the week, their marching had improved considerably and they knew the flag would be flying over their barracks by Sunday.

Saturday night, Lou was on his knees scrubbing the head when he heard someone call, "Hey, Dyson."

He looked up and saw Red coming toward him saying, "You gonna be long? I gotta use the head."

"Hey, don't let me stop ya. Go do what ya gotta do."

Red kicked the soap away from Lou before heading to the farthest urinal. "You missed a spot over here," he laughed.

Lou stood and started to walk over to get the soap and just then slipped on the soapy deck and went down hard. "Oww!" he yelled. "I think I sprained my ankle, Red. Help me up."

"Just a minute."

Red flushed the urinal and held out his hand to Lou who attempted to stand, but quickly fell back on the wet tile. "I have to finish this job. Will ya help me, O'Reilly, so I can get off my ankle?"

"Sure, I feel partly to blame for kicking the soap away from you. Let's hurry up before Clarke sees me helping you."

By Sunday, Lou could hardly stand on his left foot, but he wasn't about to let the pain interfere with his duties. He wrapped his ankle tight with a bandage Red had confiscated from sick bay and pulled his pant leg down to cover it. All too soon, it was time to assemble for marching drill, the one that would earn their barracks the Rooster flag.

Lou took his place and stepped off. Left, right, left, right. *I can do this,* he thought. They came near the reviewing stand, the white flag with the rooster emblem flying high in anticipation of its new owners, when Lou felt his ankle give out. As the pain ran up his leg, Lou began to limp out of step with his company and finally fell to the ground writhing in pain.

They did not get the Rooster flag and, to put it mildly, Petty Officer Clarke was not pleased. Lou could hardly hear what the Petty Officer was yelling because he was too busy telling himself, *you screwed up again, Lou. When are you ever going to do anything right?*

Chapter Forty-One

With proper care and medicine, Lou's ankle began to heal and, thankfully, the bulk of their third week of training was spent at the indoor pool. According to Clarke, "If you're going to be on a ship in the middle of the Pacific, you damn well better be able to swim, just in case."

The first lessons were basic, from dog paddle to side stroke to determine who could swim and who couldn't. Eric was afraid of the water and had never swum in his life, being from the streets of New York City with only a fire hydrant to keep him cool in the summer instead of a swimming pool. Lou passed the initial tests with flying colors and then rested his foot while he watched Eric and the others learn to swim.

The next day, they were given a Swim Skills Assessment that measured their ability to swim fifteen yards in chest-deep water, swim another fifteen yards in water over their heads, tread water for one full minute and float face down for one full minute. Again, Lou got the highest score in his company. His ankle was weightless in the water so it gave him no trouble.

Walking back to the locker room, his towel slung over his shoulder, Lou heard Eric running up to him. "Wait up, Aquaman. How'd you learn to swim so well?"

Lou grinned at being called one of his heroes. "I grew up on the Sound, Carlson. I've been swimming since I was little and was a lifeguard for four years."

167

"No fooling? No wonder you swim like a fish. My only hope is that I don't fall overboard 'cause if I did, I'd surely drown."

"No, you wouldn't; I'd save ya."

On the third day of that week, the recruits had to jump into deep water from a ten-foot platform. Petty Officer Clark showed them the proper way to jump by standing tall, head held high, legs crossed at the ankle and arms crossed over their chest.

"Use your inside arm to pinch your nose," he said, "bracing your hand by placing your pinky under your jaw. Do you know why we do that?"

"No sir!"

"So you don't lose your grip from the impact of hitting the water. You got that?"

"Aye, aye, sir!"

It took a while for Eric to jump, but with encouragement from Lou and bellowing from Clarke, he made it.

On the fourth day, they had to prove they could swim fifty yards without stopping or holding onto the side of the pool, all the while demonstrating the proper technique in the crawl, breaststroke, and backstroke. They had to know the proper kick for each stroke and how to exhale under water.

On Friday, they learned techniques to stay afloat while waiting for rescue. After that came the inflation test, filling their shirt and trousers with air and staying close to the surface without moving.

Petty Officer Clarke growled, "Struggling and sinking are not allowed. You snails got that?"

"Aye, aye, sir!"

Marching drills were part of every day's schedule and by Sunday, Lou was determined that his company would win the Rooster flag, not only for Clarke but for his company. He wasn't about to let them down again. Through gritted teeth he stepped sharply past the reviewing stand and when they were finally told to, "Halt," the Rooster flag was awarded to them with great ceremony.

Petty Officer Clarke almost smiled as he accepted the flag and proudly flew it from the barracks. "Do you snails know what flying this flag means?" he barked.

"Yes sir, we earned it, sir" chorused the men.

"It means that for one week you snails get to go to the front of the chow line and strut and crow at everyone else as you pass them. Can you do that?"

"Aye, aye, sir."

"I said can you do that?"

"Aye, aye, sir!"

Chapter Forty-Two

By the fourth week, the recruits started their hands-on training of knot tying, first aid techniques, and artificial respiration.

Then came the moment they were finally issued an M1 rifle. Petty Officer Clarke held up a rifle and barked, "This weapon is going to be your best friend. You'll sleep with it, eat with it, march with it, crawl with it, jump with it, hold it over your heads 'til you think your arms will break. Your weapon weighs ten pounds, but I guarantee you that at the end of the day it will feel like a lot more than that. You will pretend this is your girlfriend back home and guard it with your life. Love it. Cherish it. At the end of the week I expect each of you to know your weapon inside and out as well as you know the dimple on your girl's back. You'll need to be able to take it apart and put it back together with your eyes closed. Snails, come get your rifles."

Aye, aye, sir!!"

The fifth week of boot camp taught them firefighting and shipboard damage control. At the end of a busy day, Lou settled on his bunk and wrote a letter to his parents.

Dear Mom and Dad (and yeah, you girls, too),

You wouldn't believe what we've done these past two weeks (although I guess <u>you</u> would, Dad). Last week we were issued our rifles along with a week of weapons training, firearm safety, and live fire training. I'm not great at hitting a bullseye, but I can do it more often than not, now.

One day this week we had gas chamber training. With masks on, we were put into a room filled with gas, then were told to take off our masks. Don't worry, Mom, I didn't pass out or anything. I did throw up, but so did everyone else. Fresh air never felt so good! Then we had firefighting training in case there's a fire once we're on a ship. We had to escape a smoke-filled compartment, open and close watertight doors, use breathing apparatus, carry fire hoses (they're heavy), and extinguish fires. They actually started a fire and we had to put it out, just like real firemen.

I'm proud to be an important part of something. Fighting fires, like everything else we've learned, is based on team work and if I don't hold up my end, the whole mission fails. We're learning that each of us is part of something bigger than us and carrying out our individual duties assures success in our overall objective. You know what I mean, Dad.

Always there's marching and physical training and now we're doing those while carrying our rifles. I have muscles like I never thought possible. You'd be hard pressed to tell the difference between me and Johnny Weissmuller. Ha ha.

Seriously, I'm proud to be here and can't wait until I'm assigned to a ship. Next week we take aptitude tests to determine what our duties will be once we're on a ship. I hope I get to be an airplane mechanic.

By the way, we had our pictures taken in our uniforms this week. You should be getting one, soon.

Missing you, Lou

P.S. I graduate at the end of next week. I'll understand if you can't make it here. It's a long way away and in the middle of winter. I'll have two weeks leave after graduation so I'll be home before you know it.

Chapter Forty-Three

The final week of boot camp was a flurry of drills and tests and more marching, all in preparation for Pass-in-Review, or graduation, at the end of the week.

At 1400 hours on Tuesday, Lou was called to a room to be tested for his skills and placement. He was delighted when it was determined that he qualified as an aviation machinist's mate and would work in the hangar bay of a carrier, keeping the planes repaired. He passed Red in the hall. "What've they got you doing?" Lou asked.

Red tried to look disappointed, but was too happy to pull it off. "I'll be an aviation radio technician, Lou! It's just what I wanted. How about you? Did they figure out you're an A-1 mechanic?"

"They did, I'll be an aviation machinist's mate! Have you heard about Danny or Eric?"

"Eric hasn't been tested yet, but Danny's gonna be a fireman. Said he's wanted to be a fireman since he was little."

"Good for him. Here comes Eric now. Hey, Swanson, did they figure out what you're good at? I hope it's something besides peeling potatoes?"

"Ha ha, funny boy. Laugh now, but you won't be laughing once we're on board a ship."

"Why?" asked Red, "Did they make you an admiral?"

"Not quite. And I'm not gonna be a pilot like I wanted, either; instead, the Navy in its infinite wisdom decided they needed a yeoman which means I'll be in charge of your records. So, who's laughing now?"

The four of them walked down the hall, laughing and sparring with each other, anticipating tomorrow's twelve-hour Battle Stations testing.

Laura paced the living room, keeping her eyes focused on the front walk. *Where is that mailman?* she fumed, stubbing out one cigarette and lighting another. Soon she saw him coming up the walk and opened the door before he could put the mail in the box. "I'll take it, Kenny," she said, reaching for the mail.

He smiled. "Looks like ya got a letter from Lou today. I surely do like to deliver this kind of mail 'cause it makes my customers happy. I see ya got your blue star flag up now; that makes twenty-two homes on my route sporting one. Don't wanna see no gold stars, nosiree. Have a good day Miz Dyson."

Laura ran into the house and tore open the envelope that bore her son's handwriting. Pulling out the thin sheets of paper, she sank onto a kitchen chair, laid her cigarette in the ashtray, and took a sip of coffee, ready to inhale Lou's words.

Dear Mom and Dad,

Yay, basic training is almost over. Yesterday we had what they call Battle Stations. It started early in the morning with P.O. Clarke yelling, "Rise and shine, you snails! Man your battle stations!" Then we had twelve

174

hours of testing on all the things we've learned in these last five weeks. It was hands-on testing in swimming (of course I passed), survival, firefighting, damage control, rescue, and a bunch of other things. It was tough, but I think I passed 'em all.

Did I tell you they qualified me to be an aviation machinist which is just what I wanted? I can't wait to start fixing planes. They said I'll be assigned to the USS Hornet, an aircraft carrier! Yahoo!

We're now practicing for Pass-In-Review (that means graduation from boot camp). At that point, we'll no longer be raw recruits, we'll be real sailors. I'll have two weeks at home before I go to Norfolk to report for duty on the Hornet.

I'm looking forward to seeing you and having one of your apple pies. What do you hear from Ned and Joe? I can't wait to surprise Gus by showing up at the garage.

Your loving son,

Lou

Chapter Forty-Four

Mike walked in the door and Laura waved Lou's letter in his face. "Read this," she said, "then we can talk."

Mike took the letter and started reading it before taking off his coat and boots. When he finished, Laura was grinning, her eyes gleamed, and she could barely sit still. She was holding the picture of Lou in his uniform that had come two days earlier.

"That's my boy," he said. "So what's got you looking like you just won a blue ribbon at the fair?"

Laura helped him pull his boots off. "I've got it all worked out. It's close to the end of February and we still have gas ration coupons left so—"

"So?"

"So, we should be able to drive to Great Lakes and be there in time to see Lou graduate, then bring him home with us so he won't have to take a bus. What d'ya think? Can we do it?"

"You miss him, don't you?"

"Even more than I missed you when you were in the service. Can we?"

"Lemme think about it for a minute."

Laura went into the kitchen to prepare dinner, but after a few minutes, peeked into the living room to see if Mike had made a decision yet. Disappointed to see no change in him, she turned back to the stove and tried to concentrate on dinner.

The girls came home and they all found their places at the table. When the blessing was over, Laura could contain herself no longer so, looking squarely at Mike, she said, "Mike, what's the answer? Can we go?"

Mike put down his fork and wiped his mouth, all in exceedingly slow motion, and finally said, "Yes."

"Go where?" asked Emma, looking at her mom, then her dad.

Laura jumped up and threw her arms around Mike's neck. Then looking at the girls, said, "Your dad and I are going to drive to Great Lakes to see your brother graduate! I wish you girls could go, too, but we can't afford to feed and put up all of us on the way up and back. We'll bring Lou back with us and you'll see him soon enough."

Anna said, "I understand. We'll get the house ready to surprise him. Make sure you take pictures of his graduation."

Laura frowned. "I will, if I can figure out how that darn camera works."

Lou adjusted his cap and checked his uniform. "Hey Carlson, you ready to graduate?"

Eric nodded as he ran outside to find his parents. Lou was happy that Danny, Eric and Red's parents would be in the stands watching their sons graduate. He understood how expensive it would be for his parents to come and he knew he'd be seeing them soon, but it still hurt to know he'd have no family watching the biggest moment of his life. Reluctantly, he took a final check of his bunk and packed sea bag and headed outside.

Walking by the barracks, he heard, "Hey, Aquaman, you know these people?"

Lou turned and saw Eric and the two people he was with. "Mom! Dad!" he shouted. "You came!" Lou ran and hugged his parents as tears of happiness streamed down his face. He quickly swiped at his cheeks, knowing it was unmilitary to cry. "I'm so glad you guys are here. Mom and Dad, this is Eric. Eric, these are my folks, Mike and Laura Dyson!"

Hugs were given all around, then Lou showed his parents where to go before having to run off with Eric to get ready to graduate with their unit.

When the last recruit had passed in review and the final speech was given, the visitors swarmed the frosty field looking for their particular sailor. Mike said, "We'd be better off standing here and waiting for Lou to come to us, rather than searching through all these guys that look alike."

Laura agreed, then yelled, "I see him! He's coming over here."

Lou headed toward her surrounded by a mix of sailors and civilians. When they got close, Lou introduced his parents to Danny and Red and their parents. "And you know Eric; and these are his parents."

There was hand shaking all around with gloved hands. "Nice to meet you," said Mike. "What d'ya say we get inside out of the wind and snow flurries." The small group hurried into a building where refreshments and hot coffee awaited them. They found a table and Laura sat, but she couldn't take her eyes off her son. He looked handsome in his uniform, standing erect with his friends until the parents were seated. He seemed self-assured and confident, an unusual look for him. Then the boys left to get coffee and bring it back to the table where Lou handed a cup to Laura. She was speechless and could only smile at him, her eyes sparkling and saying what her heart felt but her voice was unable to put into words.

Mr. Epstein cradled his cup in his big hands, commenting on the fact the cups had no handles. "Strange," he muttered.

Danny explained to the group, "The cups stack better when they have no handles. Take up less room."

Mr. Epstein raised his cup and blew on the hot liquid. "Where do you guys go from here? Danny tells me he's been assigned to the Enterprise. Anyone else going on her?"

"I'm afraid not," said Eric. "Me, Red and Lou are all assigned to the new carrier, the USS *Hornet*. Sure wish Danny was coming with us, though. Fighting fires is child's play to him."

Laura took out her Brownie box camera and asked Lou's friends to pose with their parents, then with Lou. With the first two shots, she realized her hands were shaking so badly there was no way she could get a decent picture. Calming herself down, she asked everyone to pose again and this time the camera held still. She wound the camera to the end, took out the used film, and inserted a new roll of film.

Lou set his empty cup down. "When you're ready Mom, Dad, I'd like to show you around before we leave."

Mike and Laura stood, put their coats on, and said goodbye to everyone. Lou opened the door against the strong wind and escorted them around the base pointing out his barracks, the Rooster Flag which now hung over another barracks, and finally taking them to the chapel. At every stop, Laura snapped pictures to be later mounted in a photo album. Once inside the chapel, Laura said, "How peaceful it is in here. So far away from any thought of war."

"I know," said Lou, "I like to come here to think, maybe offer up a quick prayer, and just be alone for a few minutes. The chaplain has certainly helped some of us deal with being away from home for the first time."

Laura gave Lou a hug. Mike looked at his watch. "If you're ready son, I think we ought to start heading back to Connecticut before the weather gets any worse."

"I'm ready. Everything's packed in my sea bag; I'll get it and meet you in the parking lot."

Chapter Forty-Five

In the car, Lou settled on the back seat and began talking nonstop about his friends and his boot camp experience while miles of scenery flew by. Before long, Laura noticed he was stretched out on the seat, his sea bag acting as a pillow, and was fast asleep. She reached over the seat and laid a travel blanket over him, happy to have her little boy back, for a few moments at least. At a roadside diner, they woke him to have dinner, then found a nearby motor lodge to spend the night.

Late the next day the Dyson's car pulled into their driveway in New Haven. Lou looked up to see a big WELCOME HOME sign hanging over the front door. He broke into a smile, ran up the steps, and hurried inside where he found his sisters standing with arms outstretched ready to receive a hug. They were not disappointed. Lou picked up Anna and twirled her around the room, then did the same with Emma.

"Whoa!" said Emma. "Look how strong our baby brother has gotten!"

Lou looked around the living room at the red, white, and blue crepe paper streamers hanging from the ceiling and a big WE MISSED YOU sign on the wall and said, "Annie and Em, you have no idea how much I've missed you. Getting picked on by my petty officer wasn't the same as getting picked on by you two. Oh look, there's my picture! Not bad, if I do say so myself." Lou turned quiet for a moment wondering how Larry would have looked in his smartly-pressed uniform.

Lou heard someone cough and looked up. Sitting in the corner was a person he knew well.

"Mr. Gus!" he shouted and ran to him. "What a sight for sore eyes you are! How're you doing? How are Gus Jr. and Karl? Are they majors in the Army yet? Wow, I've missed you."

"I've missed you, too, Chief. Hasn't seemed the same without you hanging around the garage pestering me to teach ya somethin'. Look at you, all grown up. The Navy must be agreeing with you. Ya?"

"Ya, Gus. Thanks to you, I'm gonna be working on airplanes!"

"No kidding? Well, I knew all along you had a aptitude fer mechanics. I'm happy fer ya."

Hope started to sing, sensing that the family was back together and all was right. Hearing the canary, Gus swiped at his face with the back of his hand and turned away.

Lou put his arm around his mother. "Boy, have I missed your cooking."

"I thought you might. That's why I baked an apple pie before we left. Could you handle a piece of pie with a glass of cold milk?"

"You bet! You're the best, Mom. I told all the guys about your cooking and your blue ribbons."

"You didn't!"

"I sure did. They all envy me. Gus, have a piece of pie."

The next morning, Laura heard Lou up and about in his room and went upstairs to make his bed. She walked through his open door and stopped short when she saw Lou dressed and standing next to his tightly-made bed. "You made your bed, honey?"

"No, Mom. I made my bunk. No big deal." Laura shook her head at the change in her son. Six weeks ago, he was a boy, now a man stood before her.

Two weeks went by quickly as Lou met with friends, sat at the table with his family and enjoyed the familiarity of it all, and above all, got to sleep in until eight o'clock and awake without a bugle blaring.

One day he pulled his sisters on a sled through an empty lot and then threw a snowball at them which turned into an all-out snowball fight. The twins' aim was nothing like his and it soon proved to be too one-sided so they gave up and built a snowman instead. Lou put his sailor hat on the snowman and arranged its arm in a saluting position. The girls and Lou saluted him back and headed back to the house for hot coffee. Over the steaming liquid, Anna and Emma brought Lou up to date on Ned and Joe's whereabouts and how after basic training in North Carolina, their boyfriends were now at the Air Corps Training Center at Maxwell Field in Alabama, on their way to becoming pilots. "For now," said Anna, "we relish their letters, but we know as soon as they're trained and get deployed, we won't hear much from them."

Another day, Lou went to the garage and spent the day talking with Gus who told him that Gus Jr. and Karl were in Europe, but beyond that, he didn't know much. "Understandably," he said, "the Army's reluctant to reveal any specific information."

Gus pointed to a lump in the corner of the garage covered with a tarp. "Chief," he said, "I need ya to show me how to fix this here motorcycle, it's not braking right and you're the bike expert, not me." Lou beamed with pride, finally able to teach Gus something.

As welcome as the time home was, Lou looked forward to getting back with Red and Eric and on a ship where they could put into practice the skills they'd learned in boot camp.

With hugs all around, he said goodbye to his family and Gus, and stepped aboard the bus that would take him to Norfolk and to his unknown future. What war would be like, he could only imagine, but he was ready. And above all, he was ready to fight the Japs and win the war for America.

Chapter Forty-Six

Lou stepped off the bus at the Norfolk Naval Shipyard and gazed up at the ships lining the waterfront. Someone punched his arm and he turned to see Red standing next to him. Lou asked, "Can you believe the size of these ships?"

"Uh uh. We'll probably get lost on the *Hornet* and they won't find our bodies 'til the war's over."

"Well, let's go. This is what we trained for." Lou and Red hoisted their sea bags and proceeded up the *Hornet*'s gangway. Entering the Quarterdeck, they smartly turned aft and saluted the flag, then turned and saluted the Officer of the Day.

"Permission to come aboard," said Lou.

"Do you have your orders?"

"Yes, sir! Right here."

"Permission granted."

Lou stared at the immensity of the carrier and suddenly felt more insignificant than usual. Finding his way to the Administrator's Office to turn in his paperwork, his thoughts turned to Jonah being swallowed by a great fish. *I think I know how he felt,* he mused. Inching his way through a narrow hallway with Red right behind him, they bumped into Eric. "Hey, it's the yeoman!" cried Lou.

"Dyson! O'Reilly! Did ya see the size of this ship? I may just stay right here 'til the end of the war, 'cause if I go up on deck, I'll never find my way back."

"It sure is a tight squeeze," agreed Lou. They finished their business at the office and were given their bunk assignments and a quick overview tour of the ship. The three men followed the directions down the steep ladders to the living quarters.

"Ah, here's my bunk," said Lou. "You two find your bunks, then we'll see if we can find the mess hall and grab something to eat while the rest are still boarding."

Their first few days on board the *Hornet* were spent getting used to the ship while it remained in port. Lou was blown over by the size of the hangar bay and the number of airplanes it could hold—fighters, bombers, scout planes, torpedo bombers – 97 planes in all. He'd never seen so much aircraft in one place and he couldn't wait to learn how to repair them and begin his duties as an aviation machinist's mate.

On March 3, 1942, the crew of the *Hornet* learned they'd be leaving port the next morning and that all men were expected to be in uniform and lined up along the rail of the flight deck for the ship's departure. Lou learned they would be heading to San Francisco by way of the Panama Canal and he couldn't wait to get underway.

The trip to the West Coast would take sixteen days, giving the new sailors time to get used to living on water in a self-contained metal village, and time for Lou to learn the basics of his new trade. And on top of that, he'd get to see the Panama Canal that he'd read about in Life Magazine. *New Haven was never like this!*

The next day, March 4, while standing on deck and watching the shoreline fade into the distance, Lou suddenly felt an overwhelming pride for his country. Once out on the open sea, the sight of airplanes practicing takeoffs and landings on the flight deck filled him with inexplicable awe. He had a high respect for the mechanics involved in such operations and, as well, greatly admired the skill of the pilots.

Stretched across the flight deck of the carrier were arresting wires there for one purpose, to snag the tailhooks of the planes and bring the planes to a stop before going off the end of the ship. Lou was astonished to learn that a fifty-four-thousand-pound plane travelling a hundred and fifty miles an hour could stop in only two seconds.

The hydraulic elevators that transported the planes from the flight deck to the hangar bay, two flights down, was another marvel in mechanics. The hangar bay was where Lou spent his work day.

On the day the *Hornet* entered the Panama Canal, Lou spent his free time on the flight deck watching the locks lift the ship up and down as the carrier threaded its way through the inland route. He took out the notebook he kept in his pocket and wrote about the mechanical marvel and included a rough sketch of how the locks worked and added, *"I joined the Navy to see the world and so far, I'm definitely not disappointed."*

187

Chapter Forty-Seven

March 20, 1942. The USS *Hornet* arrived at the Naval Air Station in Alameda, California. For the next few days, scuttlebutt was ripe with news that something huge was about to happen. Talk among the crew was that Captain Mitscher had big plans for the *Hornet*. The longer the ship stayed in port, the more the rumors flew and grew.

Finally, by the afternoon of April 1, sixteen additional B-25s were loaded on the flight deck along with a hundred and thirty Army Air Corps officers and enlisted men. The *Hornet* crew was abuzz with rumors that Lieutenant Colonel James Doolittle was aboard. The next day, the *Hornet* departed Alameda under sealed orders.

Once the ship was underway, Captain Mitscher announced over the loudspeaker that their mission was a bombing raid on Japan. "America is finally going to get even with Japan for what it did to us." Rumors turned to downright excitement as the men of the *Hornet* readied themselves for action.

Lou was in the hangar bay lying under a plane's belly when he heard someone talking nearby. He rolled out from under the plane and found himself next to Col. Doolittle. Lou stood erect and saluted him and Col. Doolittle returned the salute, smiled, and said, "Here, sailor, help me a minute." Lou soon realized that medals which had been presented to U. S. sailors by Japanese dignitaries were now being attached to a five-hundred-pound bomb. It was Doolittle's intention to return the medals to Japan, by air mail, so to speak.

Lou anxiously awaited mess call so he could tell Red that the renowned pilot had not only talked with him, but had asked for his help.

On April 13, the *Hornet* joined up with the aircraft carrier *Enterprise* and with their accompanying task force, turned toward Japan. The plan was to sail within 500 miles of Japan so Col. Doolittle and his Raiders could take off from the carrier and bomb Tokyo. But their plan didn't go as scheduled. On April 18, the task force was spotted by a Japanese patrol boat and Col. Doolittle was forced to launch prematurely, nearly seven hundred miles out.

As the *Hornet* came about, a large gale churned the sea causing thirty foot crests. The ship pitched violently in the heavy swells; sea spray covered the bow soaking the flight deck and crew. Lou retired to the head where he stayed until his stomach finally settled. Red told him later that Doolittle timed his takeoff with the rise and fall of the ship's bow and soon all sixteen of his planes were in the air. Col. Doolittle tipped his wing to the *Hornet* before heading for Tokyo and America's first air strike against Japan.

The *Hornet* brought her own planes up to the flight deck and the ship sailed full speed for Pearl Harbor. At the evening mess, Red, Lou, and Eric heard over the loudspeaker that the Doolittle raid was a success. The cheer from the crew and officers was deafening.

The *Hornet* arrived at Pearl Harbor on April 25. In the few days he had before departing again, Lou got off the ship and set foot on Oahu. Looking to the east, he saw the iconic shape of Diamond Head appearing stalwart and indestructible. Glancing around him, he saw signs in abundance of devastation and war. Charred and vacant buildings sat empty, their gaping holes staring out toward the oil-covered sea. Steel debris dotted the land, eerie souvenirs of planes and battleships that had been bombed in the attack. The sound of banging and clanging from ships able to be repaired rose above the sound of the waves crashing against the shore. Lou thought back to when he heard the news of the Pearl Harbor attack on the radio. At that time, he was sitting safely in New Haven, now he was standing on the spot where it had happened. The full import of the event hit him that what he was looking at was more than a news item, it was tangible evidence of evil.

Chapter Forty-Eight

April 30, 1942. The *Hornet* departed Pearl Harbor and headed for the Coral Sea and on May 4, the ship crossed the equator. In his notebook, Lou wrote: *Today I went from a Pollywog to a Shellback, a ritual that sailors do when they cross the equator. Captain Mitscher dressed up as King Neptune and allowed the Shellbacks, those who've crossed the equator before, to feed the Pollywogs, that's us, chipped beef on toast, (what the veteran sailors call SOS) off the floor. Then we were made to put our clothes on backwards and crawl through a bunch of obstacles and then kiss King Neptune's bare foot that was covered with grease. After all that, we were officially declared to be Shellbacks. I even have a certificate to hang on the wall when I get home.* Lou put the notebook in his pocket, laid back and smiled, reliving the day's camaraderie.

Lou gave another swift kick to the dented vending machine that had swallowed his last nickel. As he stood there grumbling, a pilot in line for the machine said, "You done with the machine, seaman? I'd like to get a candy bar."

Lou turned his head and saluted the man, then said, "Go ahead. It took my last nickel, maybe you'll have better luck." He kicked it one more time for good measure. "Damn machine!"

The pilot inserted a nickel, pushed a button, and a candy bar dropped down. "Well looky that," he said, "I must have the magic touch." Then he tossed a nickel to Lou and said, "Here, seaman. What's your name?"

"Dyson, sir, Lou Dyson. And thanks."

"Don't mention it. I'm Ensign George Gay. Nice to meetcha."

"You, too. See ya around." Lou put the nickel in his pocket and walked back to the hangar bay.

The *Hornet* eventually sailed back to Pearl Harbor then, near the end of May, set out for the open sea again. During this time, Lou stuck close to the chief machinist in an effort to learn all he could about airplanes. The Doolittle raid impressed on him that a pilot is only as good as his plane, so it was crucial that the planes stay in top working order.

On June 4, the *Hornet* arrived at Midway Island with two other carriers, the *Yorktown* and the *Enterprise,* ready to do battle with the Japanese and four Jap carriers. The first torpedo squadron's fifteen planes flew off the *Hornet's* flight deck into a hail of bullets. One plane after another was shot down, having no fighter escorts to assist them. The last plane to be shot down was piloted by Ens. George Gay. With his gunner dead and himself wounded, he left his sinking plane and floated in the water hiding under a seat cushion. From his vantage point, he witnessed the dive bombing attacks by the Americans and cheered and hollered with every hit as one by one the Japanese carriers were sunk. Once darkness settled over the water, he inflated his raft and awaited help. After being in the water for some thirty hours, Ens. Gay was rescued and flown to a ship for treatment of his wounded left hand.

Word quickly spread through the hangar bay that all fifteen planes of the torpedo squadron, each carrying two men, had been shot down. Lou knew that Ens. Gay had piloted one of those planes and fingered the nickel in his pocket to calm his fears. The next day, news of Ens. Gay's rescue brought cheers from the crew; however, the news was tempered by the fact that of the thirty-man squadron, Ens. Gay was the lone survivor. Lou put the nickel he'd given him in a safe place and vowed he'd never spend it.

When they returned to Oahu, a new captain took over as commanding officer of the *Hornet*. The ship spent the next eight weeks in port stocking up on supplies, making minor repairs, and adding new anti-aircraft guns.

Finally, on August 17, the *Hornet* sailed back into the war zone. A week later, the *Enterprise* suffered bomb damage, then the *Saratoga* was torpedoed, and on September 15 the *Wasp* was sunk, causing the captain to announce, "Gentlemen, the USS *Hornet* is the only operational US carrier in the South Pacific for now. It is up to us to provide air cover for the Solomon Islands."

Once the *Enterprise* was repaired, it rejoined the *Hornet* and on October 26 the two carriers and their escorts were stationed off the Santa Cruz Islands. Before dawn that morning Lou awoke to, "Man your battle stations!" At 0900, they were told to expect a large number of Japanese bombers. At 0930, twenty-six planes came into view and were shot down over the next few hours. During the second wave of attack, which lasted nearly fifteen minutes, the *Hornet* was hit by three dive bombers. All hands, including Lou, were on deck putting out fires using hoses and bucket brigades. One of the dive bombers, being heavily damaged by the *Hornet's* new anti-aircraft guns, crashed into the *Hornet*, killing seven men. Burning gas spread over the flight deck. Firemen pulled hoses and battled ceaselessly to put out the fires. When it looked as though the situation was somewhat under control, two torpedoes hit the ship, seriously damaging the electrical systems and engines. Lou looked up in time to see a wounded torpedo plane crash into the *Hornet's* side, causing even more damage.

With no power, the carrier was unable to launch or land aircraft so a nearby cruiser towed the carrier clear of the action while enemy planes continued their attack against the *Enterprise*. Then a torpedo scored a fatal hit on the *Hornet's* starboard side, causing her to list.

"Abandon ship!" came the order at 1700. "Grab your life jackets. You have two minutes to get in the water!" Lou scrambled to the edge of the deck and helped calm his fellow sailors as they dropped into the cold, oily sea. Wounded men were airlifted from one ship to another with the use of litters and ropes.

"Lou, help me!" came a familiar voice. Lou turned to see Eric. His face was ashen and his body trembling. "I'm scared. I don't wanna jump into the ocean."

"You have to," said Lou. "You'll be alright, you have your life jacket on and I'll be right beside you. Remember how we were taught to jump? Hands over chest, holding your nose and bracing your chin with your pinky?"

Eric nodded gravely.

"Okay then, at the count of three, we'll jump. Ready? One, two, three!"

The two men jumped off the *Hornet* into the dark sea. Lou stayed with Eric, talking nonstop to calm him until they were picked up by a nearby destroyer. Eric's face was bloodied from his nose breaking when he hit the water; otherwise, Yeoman Carlson would live to serve his country another day.

After more than 2500 men aboard the *Hornet* had left the ship, the captain was the last man to leave, knowing that a hundred and forty of his men had lost their lives that day at Santa Cruz. Once aboard another ship, the captain reluctantly ordered what was left of the USS *Hornet* to be sunk.

Lou was transferred to the *Enterprise,* Red and Eric went to other ships and Lou never saw them again.

Chapter Forty-Nine

Mike and Laura walked back into the house after the Sunday church service. There had been a special prayer that morning for the men and women serving in the war.

Laura peeled off her gloves and sputtered, "I can't believe they're now allowing women into the war. First the WAACs now the WAVES. What is Roosevelt thinking of? Next thing you know, the women will be in combat next to the men." Laura trembled. "I certainly don't want Lou's life to be dependent on some delicate little missy fighting next to him."

Mike kissed her forehead. "Don't worry about it, honey. I'm sure they plan on using them as nurses or office personnel, some place far away from combat."

"Well I certainly hope so."

"Tell me, what's really bothering you?"

"Oh, hon, it's Lou. We don't hear anything from him and have no idea where his ship is. I understand he can't tell us anything, loose lips sink ships and all, but I read about so many ships sinking that I have nightmares of him being on one of them."

Mike held her tightly. "Remember, no news is good news. If something happened to Lou, we'd have men on our doorstep letting us know. As long as we don't hear anything, it means nothing bad has happened." He lifted her chin. "Feel better?"

"No. Not 'til he comes home in one piece."

Mike went into the living room to read the Sunday paper while his wife made lunch. He turned right to the war news and what he read sent shivers down his back. At that moment, he had to decide if he should tell Laura that the USS *Hornet* had sunk in the Pacific. He decided to wait since it had happened a week earlier and they'd had no one at their front door carrying bad news. Yet.

Chapter Fifty

Lou stepped onto the Enterprise and felt his adrenaline rush slowly subside. He stood there, looking out over the sea at the spot where the *Hornet* had been. A sense of sadness engulfed him so deeply, he had to find a place to sit before he fell. Ten months ago, he was dreaming of joining the Navy and being a part of its glory and honor. Now he was in the Navy and his world, in all its glory, was sitting on the bottom of the Pacific Ocean. Men he came to know and love were either injured or killed. He sat there, thinking about Red and Eric and sent out a quick prayer that they'd be kept safe on their new ships. Then he heard a noise behind him.

"Dyson! Is that you? I heard men and planes from the *Hornet* would be joining us. Son of a gun!"

Lou turned to see Danny, his fireman's gear and face covered with soot, wearing a smile a yard wide. "Epstein! Lookit you, doing just what you always wanted to do."

"Yeah, and I've gotta get busy again, those planes just keep bombing us. We're the last US carrier in the Pacific that's still afloat and we need to keep her that way. Catch ya later." Danny ran off.

Lou walked around the vast ship to get his bearings. The *Hornet* wasn't the only ship bombed during the Santa Cruz attack; the *Enterprise* was, too. Forty-four of her men were killed and seventy-five wounded. Despite the damage, she continued the fight against the Japanese.

Hanging proudly on the flight deck was a sign in big bold letters, declaring, "*Enterprise* vs. Japan." Lou smiled at the message that evoked the desperation yet resolve of the men serving on the beloved flattop, a ship that was now his new home.

He and the other rescued men from the *Hornet* were sent to supply to get a new sea bag, uniform, and shaving kit to replace what now lay on the ocean floor. Lou tried not to think of the pictures of his family that were lost forever.

Then he went to the ship's store and bought a new pocket notebook to record his experiences. His old one was wet and when dried out, barely readable. He transferred what notes he could remember to the new notebook, then laid his New Testament in the sun to dry out.

When the bombing stopped, the *Enterprise* sailed to New Caledonia for repairs, but before the repairs could be completed, she was needed at the Solomon Islands for a new Japanese onslaught. Seabees stayed on the ship to continue repairs, right into battle.

Lou and Danny enjoyed cups of coffee during a welcome break. Danny held his cup with two hands and said, "Can ya believe this? We're heading out to sea with air hammers still pounding and welders' arcs still sparking."

"I know. There's a big bulge in the ship's side, an oil tank is leaking, and one of the elevators to the flight deck is still jammed. Thank heavens the flight deck has three elevators or we'd be in deep trouble."

"Yeah," said Danny looking around. "I don't know which I admire most, the brave Enterprise herself or the construction battalion that's working furiously to keep her afloat while we sail. What a great ship we're on, right?"

Lou smiled at Danny. "You bet."

Before returning to New Caledonia in mid-November to finish repairs, the *Enterprise* assisted in the sinking of sixteen ships and damaging eight others. During that time, Lou spent his days in the hangar bay with the other mechanics keeping the planes up and running. On December 5, the *Saratoga* was repaired and back in battle, meaning the *Enterprise* was no longer the only carrier defending the Pacific.

Chapter Fifty-One

1943 started with the sun rising over the New Hebrides where the crew of the *Enterprise* had been based for a month, ready to go where needed. A few days later, they sailed to the Solomon Islands where they successfully destroyed Japanese bombers. From there, the carrier sailed to Espiritu Santo where it stayed docked for three months.

In late May, scuttlebutt was rampant that something exciting was about to happen. Ens. Howard Mason approached Danny, wiping his face with a towel after a calisthenics workout on the flight deck. Danny was out of breath, but Ens. Mason, lithe and athletic, had barely broken a sweat. "Epstein," Mason said, "have you heard the news? Word's out that Captain Ginder's sending us back to Pearl to get some sort of a citation."

"Swell. It'll be great to be on American soil again."

As they steamed into the harbor, the men lined the rail of the flight deck. Soon, with much pomp and circumstance, Admiral Nimitz came aboard and presented the USS *Enterprise* with the first Presidential citation ever awarded an aircraft carrier. Lou and the rest of the men burst with pride, knowing they each had had a part in earning that award.

Danny squeezed through the hangar bay looking for Lou. It was mid-summer and not a lot of air circulated between the planes. He found Lou leaning against a plane's tail downing a Coke. "Ah, there you are."

"What brings you down here?" asked Lou. "You slumming?"

"I must be, I found you, didn't I? Gimme a swig of that soda and I'll tell you what the latest rumor mill is spewing out."

"Here, finish it. So, what's up?"

Danny wiped his mouth with his sleeve. "I just heard that other American carriers have joined the Pacific fleet."

"Great, but so what?"

"So, the *Enterprise* has been relieved of duty and being sent to Bremerton base in Washington for an overhaul. Heaven knows it needs one. It'll be gone four months while it gets some upgrades and, get this, a torpedo bulge."

"What the heck is a torpedo bulge?"

"From what Mason tells me, it's a water-filled compartment they install on either side of the hull so when a torpedo hits, it'll help detonate it and absorb the explosion."

"No kidding? They can do that? Wait, what do we do while the ship's in Washington for four months?"

"We stay here, go to school, and get to enjoy the beach. Growing up in Buffalo, I had no idea there really was a paradise. But buddy, Hawaii is paradise with a capital P."

One evening after enjoying the pounding surf, Danny said, "Dyson, how about going to the USO with me? I hear they have pretty decent chow and the dames are nothing to sneeze at, either."

"Where's the USO?"

"Honolulu. Just a hop, skip and a jump from here. We can hitch a ride over."

Lou shrugged his shoulders. "Okay, I suppose we can check it out."

The two men walked into the USO Club and saw wall-to-wall people. Some were at tables eating or playing games while many others were on the dance floor swinging to a Benny Goodman song playing on the Victrola. A young woman walked over and welcomed them to the USO "Hi, my name's Sarah. Can I help you sailors find anything here?"

"Sure thing," said Danny. "I'm Danny and this is Lou and we're here to get a hot meal and meet some dame . . . uh, women."

Sarah laughed. "You've come to the right place. If you go over to that counter, they'll be happy to serve you dinner. As to the *dames*," she stressed the word, "most of us have been recruited by the local college to come here and help out. We love to dance or just sit and talk and find out where you're from, what your girl back home is like, anything you want to talk about. And if you want to write home, we have USO stationery for your use."

"Thank you," said Lou. "I don't know about you Danny, but my first order of business is to get some good cooking in me. I sure miss Mom's meals."

"A cuppa joe and a tire sound good to me," said Danny.

"A tire?" asked Sarah.

"Yeah, a donut, or maybe two or three. Danny patted his belly."

Sarah laughed and pointed to the far side of the room. "Right over there."

When they got their food and found space at a table, Danny looked around and said, "Hey, lookit, there's Mason. Man, I didn't know he could jitterbug! Mason, over here!"

The tall ensign walked over and Danny introduced him to Lou. "Mason, Lou here's a top-notch mechanic. Fixing motors or repairing planes, it's all duck soup to him."

The men shook hands and Mason went back to his dance partner, a young blond whose long pony tail swished back and forth as her body moved to the music.

Sarah brought a girl over to Danny and Lou's table, smiled at them and said, "Lou, I want you to meet Alani. She's a freshman at the University of Hawaii and is helping out here for the summer."

Danny and Lou rose to offer the girls a seat, then Lou sat spellbound as he stared at Alani's dark, dancing eyes and bright red lips. The white jasmine flower behind her right ear added stark contrast to her coal black hair. Between her looks and the sweet fragrance of the flower, Lou could do nothing but gaze at this goddess in front of him. Danny finally nudged him to snap him out of his trance and Lou managed to say, "Oh, uh, hi Alani. That's a beautiful name."

Alani smiled at him and twirled a few strands of her hair, sending Lou into another daze.

Danny rose and took Sarah's hand. "We'll leave you two to get acquainted; that is, if you remember how to talk." They walked onto the dance floor to swing and sway with Sammy Kaye.

Over the next hour, Lou and Alani talked about Hawaii, New Haven, the *Enterprise, Hornet*, college, and Mom's apple pie. By the time Danny and Sarah strolled back to their table, it was clear Lou and Alani had learned how to converse. In fact, they were so engrossed in their conversation, Danny couldn't get a word in edgewise.

"Hey Lou," he interrupted, "we gotta get back to base."

"But—"

"Nope, we gotta leave now. See you again, girls."

On their way out the door, Lou turned and saw Alani watching him so he raised his hand and blew her a kiss. She reached out to grab it and closed her delicate fingers around it.

Lou floated back to the base.

The next night Lou was shaven, hair combed, and aftershave applied, eager to get back to the USO. When he and Danny arrived, Lou scanned the room looking for his dream girl. There were so many black-haired Hawaiian girls in the room, he had to wait until they turned around to see if one was Alani. He finally found her on the dance floor with a Marine, his arms draped around her like an octopus. Lou's heart sank. Alani looked up, noticed Lou and smiled.

Lou poured himself a cup of coffee and sat gloomily at a table, trying not to hate a Marine he didn't even know. While still feeling sorry for himself, he felt a tap on his shoulder and looked up to see Alani, as beautiful as ever, standing next to him. He rose and offered her a seat which she readily accepted.

Lou was puzzled. "I thought you were with the Marine tonight."

Alani twirled her hair. "I was, for one dance. I, uh, got in trouble last night for spending so much time with my Lou. We are supposed to divide our time among all of you."

Lou took her hand. "I'm sorry. Not because you spent time with me, but because you got in trouble. Does that mean we can't spend an hour together tonight?"

Alani grinned, her pearl-white teeth sparkling. "Not all at once, but I can spend ten minutes at a time with you after talking with others for a few minutes. Will that be okay, my Lou?"

"Sure. Anything so I can see you and keep you from getting into trouble. Wanna dance?"

"I thought you'd never ask."

By the end of the evening, Lou had a phone number where he could reach Alani, knowing the September semester was about to begin and she wouldn't be spending as much time at the USO once school started.

In November, Lou made his way over to the USO without Danny. He didn't need his friend for what he had to do. A call to Alani had assured him she would be at the club waiting for him.

When he entered the door, Alani was nearby talking with two other women. Seeing Lou, she ran over and wrapped him in a warm hug. He returned the hug then suggested they sit somewhere far away from the crowd, if that was even possible. They got drinks and found a table. As much as he wanted to, Lou had trouble looking at her and found himself looking at the dance floor, the kitchen, and a nearby table where two men played cribbage.

Alani reached for his hand. "What is the matter, my Lou?"

Lou opened his mouth to speak, but no words came out. He cleared his throat and tried again. "I have . . . I have to tell you—"

"Tell me what?"

Lou looked into her dark eyes and found a little courage. "Our ship is back and we'll be going aboard tomorrow. Then we'll be sailing back into battle."

Alani eyes glistened. "So that means—"

"That means we may never see each other again," Lou blurted out. "I wish it wasn't so, 'cause, 'cause . . . I love you, Alani." Lou lifted her out of her chair, gave her a huge embrace and kissed her like there was no tomorrow. Because for them, there could well be no tomorrow.

Chapter Fifty-Two

1944. The *Enterprise* spent most of the year between being at sea and in various ports. She engaged in battles in the Marshall Islands, Truk, New Guinea, the Marianas, Saipan, Guam, the Philippines, Ulithi, Okinawa, Formosa, and Leyte. During that time, her planes and guns shot down over 900 enemy planes and bombed and sank 71 ships. The *Enterprise* even made aviation history by launching the first night radar bombing attacks from a U.S. carrier.

Planes flew off the ship in a continual assault of the islands. The hangar bay was a hectic work place, raising planes to the flight deck, then lowering returning planes for refueling and repair. The planes took off day and night with no let up, keeping the mechanics in a perpetual state of readiness.

Lou was no longer the raw recruit that graduated from boot camp. He was now a veteran of many battles and had advanced to Petty Officer. Aviation mechanics came easy to him, just as car mechanics had, and now he was teaching newer guys who came on board who didn't know a socket wrench from a monkey wrench.

On December 6, 1944, the *Enterprise* returned to Pearl Harbor. As soon as Lou was given permission to leave the ship, he headed straight to the USO. It had been a year since he'd left Alani, but he never forgot the way she looked and smelled and smiled. And the way her shapely body felt in his arms. Hoping to take up where they'd left off, Lou hurried into the club and looked around. He checked every girl there, but none were Alani.

He approached the food counter and made eye contact with the cook. "Excuse me, sir," he said, "is Alani working tonight?"

The cook looked at him with a blank stare, then slowly showed signs of recollection. "Oh, Alani, she not work here anymore. She married."

Lou grabbed the counter and held on tight to keep from falling. He felt nauseated, dizzy, his throat went dry.

"You okay?" the cook asked, pointing a ladle at him.

"Yeah. I . . . I . . . gotta go." With that, Lou ran out, vowing never to go back to the USO again. He went aboard the ship, proceeded to his bunk, and lay down, staring aimlessly at the bunk above him.

The next morning, Danny bumped into him in the chow line. "There you are, Dyson. I heard you went to the USO last night, but when I got there, I couldn't find ya. What'd you do, go off with what's her name, Alana?"

"Alani."

"My mistake, Alani. So, what was it like? Did ya need a fireman to put out the fire? I'm always available, ya know."

"Go away."

"Uh oh. Trouble in paradise?"

"Look, since you're not gonna leave me alone, let's go sit and eat the Navy's version of eggs and if you'll get me a cuppa joe, I'll tell you what happened."

"Deal. Now spill."

"She's married."

"You married her last night? You dog!"

"No, I didn't marry her. She got married while we were out at sea fighting for our country."

"Good for her. Oops, too soon, right?"

"Way too soon, dummy. I know I didn't have any claim to her, but I was sure looking forward to seeing her again."

"That stinks, man."

"Yeah it does. But I guess if she's happy, that's what counts."

"I gotta tell ya, you're handling this better than I would."

"Only on the surface, Epstein, only on the surface."

In February 1945, the ship headed for Iwo Jima to support the marines. Occasionally, pilots stuck around the hangar bay long enough to fill Lou in on what they saw as they flew over the island. Their reports confirmed for Lou that he was quite happy to be where he was and not on the ground in the midst of the action. He knew, from letters that were able to get through to him, that his parents were worried about him, but he'd tried to let them know he wasn't in the same type of immediate danger the soldiers and Marines were in. Lou was happy being on the *Enterprise*. The ship and its accompanying fleet had the reputation of ruling the Pacific against the Japanese.

Chapter Fifty-Three

April 1, 1945. Easter Sunday arrived. The First Baptist church was so packed that Mike and Laura and the girls thought they might have to sit somewhere other than in their usual pew half-way up on the left side of the church, but two strangers moved over, leaving just enough room for them to squeeze in. Laura nodded, and looked around. *So many people coming together today, and probably for more than the Easter message. I'm sure most of these people either have someone in the service or know someone who is. This dreadful war has gone on over three years and more and more gold stars are springing up in windows along our quiet streets.*

Amid the fragrance of the lilies and the warmth of the morning sun streaming through the stained-glass windows, Laura prayed fervently that she'd never have to go gold.

When they arrived home, Mike settled on the couch to read the paper and the girls went upstairs to write to Ned and Joe. Laura checked the roast she'd put in the oven before leaving for church. The savory aroma told her it was nearly done. She picked up a tomato to slice, but her hands shook so hard she had to be careful not to cut herself. An uneasy feeling had taken hold of her for days and she just couldn't shake it. She didn't want to bother the rest of the family with her silly fear; she knew she'd get through it just as she had every other time. Laura put down the knife and lit a cigarette, leaving an empty pack on the counter. Automatically, she pulled out the inside liner and started peeling away the foil, adding it to the tennis-sized ball of aluminum foil they were saving. *Compared to what the boys are doing, this is a small contribution to the war effort.*

Lou's letters home were so full of blacked out lines that all she knew for sure was that he was still alive and on some ship somewhere. She should be happy, knowing he was alive, but it was her son, confound it, and she wanted to know everything about him. Like where he was. If he was healthy. If he was happy. And especially, if he was coming home soon. The things a mother needs to know about her child.

Emma entered the kitchen with a pen and stationery in her hand. "Mom, how do you spell ammunition? How many m's and how many n's?"

Laura spelled the word in her head. "Two m's and one n. You writing to Joe?"

"Yeah. I don't know if it'll get through, but I want to let him know Anna and I are now working in a plant that makes machine gun parts. For all we know, they may be using our guns in their planes. Wouldn't that be something?"

"Yes, something," Laura shivered.

On April 12, the world was stunned to learn that President Franklin Roosevelt had died. The Dysons sat close to the radio listening to updates and the swearing in of Harry Truman as the new president. "Oh dear, oh dear," cried Laura, "I just knew something bad was going to happen. I feel sorry for Eleanor, but at least I

214

can relax knowing my anxiety had nothing to do with Lou."

Chapter Fifty-Four

Sput, sput, sput. *Uh oh,* thought Ned Andrews, *that doesn't sound good.* Ned had just dropped his bombs on Okinawa and was heading back to the USS *Bennington* when he heard the starboard engine sputter. Communication with his commanding officer cleared the way for him to land on the nearest carrier in the area.

The crew on the *Enterprise* received an alert about the emergency landing of another carrier's plane and had the arresting wires and firefighters at the ready.

"I see it," yelled Danny. "Here it comes!"

The Anna Lynn came in too high and was flagged to come around again. Ned took off and made another pass, landing successfully on the second go around. With hoses and fire extinguishers ready, the crew waved the pilot and gunner out of the plane. Five stars decorated the side of the plane.

Ned reported to the ship's captain, then made sure his plane was secured in the hangar bay for repair. Lifting a cup of black coffee to his lips, he felt someone slap him on the back. He turned around and saw a familiar face. "Lou? Is that really you?"

"In all my glory. What a surprise, having you land on our ship. How ya doing?"

"I'm fine. Just got back from dropping my load on Okinawa. I musta gotten hit in my engine." Ned looked Lou up and down. "Lookit you, here on the Big E!"

"Yup, and I'm gonna make sure your plane is ready to fly again."

"No kidding. Wait'll I tell Joe I saw you."

"You still in contact with Joe? How is he?"

"Doing great. Should be back on the *Bennington* by now. Incredibly, we've managed to be together throughout the war."

"Swell."

"So . . . I have to ask, how are Anna and Em? Any idea if they still remember us?"

"You're kidding, right? Last I heard, they're both still as crazy about you guys as ever."

Joe put an arm around Lou's shoulder and ruffled his hair. "Thank you, my brother. You made my day."

Lou jerked away. "Cut that out; I'm not a kid."

"No, no you're not. You're all grown up and serving your country well, sir."

"That's better."

Ned and Lou walked around the Anna Lynn checking her condition.

"I like the name of your plane. What did Joe name his, the Emma Lee?"

"You got it."

"Whatcha gonna do when the war's over?" asked Lou.

"Marry your sister. What about you?"

"I'm thinking of opening a motorcycle repair shop with my GI Bill. You really got me into bikes when you bought yours. Oh, here, I want ya to meet my buddy and favorite firefighter, Danny Epstein. Danny, this is my future brother-in-law, Ned Andrews."

"So you're the pilot that decided to stop in for a visit. Nice to meet ya."

"You, too. With kamikaze pilots hitting so many ships nowadays, a good firefighter is a necessity."

Lou looked at Danny. "Don't have ta tell us about kamikazes. One hit our ship recently."

"For real? What was it like?"

Danny looked at the ceiling as though he were staring into the sky, remembering. "I was up on the flight deck; Jap planes were flying around the ship and our guns were going rat-a-tat-tat-tat-tat. Spent casings were clanging against the deck, piling up like hail in a spring storm. Ink smudges from the hit planes dotted the sky and pieces of metal rained down into the water. Then this one plane managed to avoid our guns and kept coming right at us. We'd been briefed about kamikaze pilots, but seeing one was something I'll never ever forget. He kept coming closer and closer and the next thing we knew, bam! He crashed right onto our deck. We hurried around to put out the fireball that the collision had created. He'd only hit us on the side, so he didn't do much damage. We pushed what was left of him and his plane overboard."

Ned clung on every word and finally shook his head. "Unbelievable."

Lou patted Danny's arm. "I was down below, but when Danny tells the story, I'm right there on top watching the action. I may not have seen it, but I sure did hear the noise when he hit us. We were knocked off our feet for a second!"

"We were briefed," added Danny, "about kamikaze pilots and how they're not well trained and the planes they use are obsolete. Expendable issue both." Danny shook his head. "And with a fuel shortage in Japan, they only have enough fuel to get them to their target, not enough to get them back if they miss."

Ned smiled. "Makes you proud to be an American, doesn't it? I hope your mother didn't hear about that, Lou. When did you say it happened?"

"Last month, about a week or so after Easter. As a matter of fact, it was the day before President Roosevelt died. I remember they announced his death while we were still beating our gums about the crash."

Chapter Fifty-Five

Ned tipped his wing to the *Enterprise* as he and his gunner took off in their fully-repaired plane. He patted his pocket, indicating to Lou that he would deliver his letters should he make it home before Lou.

It was early May and the beginning of spring, but seasons were difficult, if not impossible, to recognize in the middle of the South Pacific surrounded by water instead of top soil and steel instead of tulips. There wasn't a fragrant lilac bush in sight. Still, Lou knew it was spring and in his mind, could picture New Haven coming out of its winter doldrums with colorful forsythia bursting forth and soft green grass appearing on lawns. And dogwood trees. An image of the graceful trees lining Park Boulevard with their white and pink flowers came into Lou's mind. He'd heard that the brown spot on each of the four petals represented the nails of the cross. Dogwood trees always reminded him of a delicate, gossamer Japanese painting. Japan. War. Lou shook his head to clear his mind and get back to work.

The following Sunday, Lou, Danny and Mason shared a table in the chow hall and talked shop until an announcement came over the loudspeaker reminding the crew that it was May 13 and they were to remember their mothers on this Mother's Day.

"No kidding?" said Mason. "Today is Mother's Day? If I were home I'd bring my mom some flowers. Yellow roses are her favorites. What about you guys?"

Danny stirred his corn into his mashed potatoes. "I'd be helping my mom out with my kid sister and little brother. She works hard at a factory all week, so I'd give her a day to rest while I took over. Yeah, I think she'd like that. Lou?"

Lou reflected on the question while he slabbed butter on a roll. Danny and Mason waited while Lou finished the process, popped the roll in his mouth, and finally swallowed. Lou smiled with thoughts of home. "My mom is probably glued to the radio right now with a pan of apples sitting in her lap waiting to be pared. She makes the best pies in the world. What would I do for her? I'd untie her apron and take her out to a restaurant where she'd get waited on hand and foot. She could order anything she wanted and wouldn't have to clean up afterwards. And . . ." Lou brushed away the liquid in the corner of his eye, "wrap my arms around her in a huge hug."

The boys raised their cups in a toast. "To mothers!"

Chapter Fifty-Six

May 14, 1945. While off Kyushu, Japan, Lou was on the flight deck at 0645, cup of coffee in hand, enjoying the momentary peace and thinking about Mother's Day the day before.

When hanging out in the hangar bay, Lou could almost convince himself he was in Gus' garage doing what he loved best. But when he took the elevator up to the flight deck, he was brought back to the realization that war was all around him. The air was usually thick with smoke, the noise deafening, and his nostrils stinging with the acrid odor of burning gasoline from direct hits on enemy planes. For now, though, all was calm.

Taking a few more sips, Lou looked toward the sky. He saw Jap planes approaching the *Enterprise* like mosquitos swarming on a warm summer evening. The carrier's guns began rattling off shells toward the planes.

Hearing a louder than usual engine noise, Lou looked around and saw a zero on course to hit the deck just a few yards away from where he was standing. For a moment he stood still and made eye contact with the pilot. He saw fear in the young man's eyes when the pilot realized he had just seconds to live.

Then Lou saw Danny standing in the plane's path, fire hose in hand.

"He's too close," thought Lou. "He'll get hit."

Lou rushed over and tackled Danny, pushing him out of the way a split second before the crash. They both landed on the deck, dazed for a second, then Danny rose and scurried away to help put out the plane's fire while Lou remained on his stomach on the deck. Suddenly a deafening boom sounded as pieces of metal and human bodies shot into the air. Lou heard cymbals crash next to his head and felt his body lift and come back down with a thud. Then everything went black.

All hell broke loose on the *Enterprise.* People rushed everywhere trying to take care of multiple situations at once. The kamikaze plane had had an eleven-hundred-pound delayed-action bomb strapped to its underside. When the plane had come in, the ship made a hard swing to the left to avoid it, but to no avail. The plane came at them at an angle and the resulting crash left a huge gaping hole in the flight deck. Then the bomb separated and penetrated the elevator pit where it detonated. The engine of the plane landed in a corner of the elevator blowing a large hole in the second deck and a smaller hole in the third. The bomb detonation hurled the fifteen-ton elevator four hundred feet into the air. Bodies were flung across the deck from the explosion. The zero's pilot was blown to pieces. While the firemen worked rapidly to put out the many fires caused by the blast, the medics scrambled over and around hoses to get the injured onto litters and down to sick bay. The kamikaze pilot had killed fourteen sailors, wounded sixty-eight, and gravely damaged the carrier. His superior officer in the Imperial Japanese Navy would be proud.

The *Enterprise* remained stable and did not list. She maintained her station in the task force formation and though wounded, continued to attack the enemy planes dotting the sky.

When the fires were fully extinguished, Danny rushed to sick bay to check on Lou. Down there he saw medical officers and assistants rushing to tend to the most severely hurt while keeping the rest comfortable until they could be treated. The room was bursting with injured men; some still lay on litters in cramped space across the deck. Danny heard moaning and an occasional scream. Searching the bedlam for Lou, he finally saw him on a litter in the corner of the room, unconscious.

He made his way through the crush of bodies to get to his friend. When he reached Lou, he saw a bloody makeshift bandage on his head meant to staunch the flow of blood until the doctors could get to him. His right arm was slashed and bloodied, a piece of steel was embedded in his skin. As much as he wanted attention for his friend, Danny knew that the men being worked on were in far worse condition. Triage, they called it, tend to the worst first.

He bowed his head and said a quick prayer for Lou, then wiped his eyes. "Lou, I'm so sorry. I hope you can hear me 'cause I need you to know it's all my fault that you're in this condition. I'd do anything if I could turn the clock back and not be in the way when that Jap hit. I owe you my life, buddy; you saved my worthless butt and I . . . well, I can never repay you for what you did. Don't you dare die on me, you hear?"

Chapter Fifty-Seven

The next day, Lou and his fellow patients in sickbay were transferred to the *Bountiful,* a nearby hospital ship. Lou remained in a coma, unaware of the damage done to the Big E or of the number of men killed and injured as a result of the pilot whose eyes he'd seen seconds before the crash.

***

Lou basked in the sun, floating on his back in Long Island Sound. It was peaceful, nothing but the gentle rocking of the waves below him and the white, fluffy clouds above. Life was beautiful, but an odd thought kept trying to interrupt his bliss. No matter, it couldn't be important. Yet there it was again. In an effort to get back to his pleasant dream, Lou fought against the intrusion. Soon he found himself moving further from paradise as black smoke began to engulf him. He could see a plane, an enemy plane coming at him. No, not at him, at Danny. "Get out of there, Danny!"

"Lou. Lou." He heard a voice calling his name.

He still couldn't speak, but his mind said, "Yes, who is it?"

"It's me, Lou. Your brother, Larry."

"Larry?"

"Yes, little brother. I've been watching over you for twenty-two years. I know you've idolized me, and wrongly so I might add, but it's important for you to know that you're my hero. What you did for Danny was selfless. You saved his life just as you saved our sisters when they fell overboard. Then you saved Karen. And Eric, too, when he was too scared to abandon ship."

"Huh?"

"Like I said, I've been with you since we were born and I couldn't be prouder to have you as my brother. I think you can handle things now, so I'll leave you to get better. Goodbye."

"Larry? Larry! Don't go."

"Dyson!"

"Larry?" Lou fluttered his eyelids and saw a bright light flooding him. Standing over him was a man all in white.

"No, Lou, it's Doctor Carbony. I'm glad to see you're awake."

"Where am I?"

"You're on the *Bountiful*, a hospital ship."

"Why? Wh . . .what happened?"

"You were knocked unconscious when the kamikaze plane hit the *Enterprise*. You've been out quite a while; good to see you're back with us."

Lou wrinkled his nose at the antiseptic smells assailing him. "How long . . . was I out?"

"A week. That gave us time to patch you up. You had a severe wound to your head and one to your arm. Your head is healing nicely, but I'm afraid the shard of

226

metal that struck your arm severed a tendon in your bicep."

Lou automatically lifted his left arm and felt the bulky bandage on his head. Then he saw another bandage on his right arm. "Am I going to be okay?"

"You will, especially once you're home with your family. This injury is your ticket home. We took the shrapnel out of your arm, but you'll be transported to a Naval hospital in Oahu for surgery on the tendon and then go through a period of rehabilitation. It's possible you'll have occasional pain and less strength in that arm for the rest of your life. But the main thing is, you're alive."

Lou closed his eyes as the scene of a week ago came rushing back to him in full force. He started with a jolt and tried to sit up. "Danny! What about Danny? Is he okay?"

The doctor nodded while laying his patient back down. If you mean the Danny that contacts us every day asking about you, yes, he's fine. He'll be relieved to know you're awake."

"My things?"

"No need to worry; your sea bag is safe with us."

Lou laid back on his pillow and allowed sleep to overtake him.

Chapter Fifty-Eight

When the *Bountiful* steamed into Pearl, Lou and the other patients were transferred by wheelchairs to the hospital where nurses in crisp white uniforms greeted them. Lou took note of the clean halls, numerous rooms and vases of hibiscus and plumeria that added bright color to the vast stretches of white walls.

Lou was wheeled to the room where he'd be staying until his medical discharge came through from the Navy. Clutched in his fist was a Purple Heart presented to him by the commander of the *Bountiful*. At the time it was awarded to him, he had tried to salute his commander, but being unable to raise his arm, his useless limb stayed put in his lap. He opened the nightstand drawer and gently laid the medal next to the New Testament which he credited with saving his life. With such damage and so many dead from the blast, it had to be the invisible force surrounding the pocket Testament that protected him. At least that's what his mother would say. And who was he to argue with his mother?

Surgery on his arm was performed later that week, then began a long period of rehabilitation. The physical therapist was ruthless, demanding more of Lou than he felt capable of giving.

"I can't do it!" he cried out on more than one occasion. "Just teach me how to use my left arm so I can go home."

"You can do it," the therapist calmly responded.

After a few more sessions of pleading to be left alone, yet still trying his hardest, Lou noticed his arm begin to loosen from its frozen position. With more therapy, he found he could lift his arm, a little at first, then higher as the weeks wore on. The relief of being able to use his arm was reflected broadly on his face.

Lou knew he'd achieved a tremendous milestone the afternoon a superior officer entered his room and he raised his arm in a salute. Going home was getting closer every day.

With Germany having surrendered, the war in Europe was basically over. Could the war with Japan be coming to a close as well? In bits and pieces, Lou knit together news of the *Enterprise* and what had happened on that fateful day. He heard about the damage inflicted to the ship and the number of men who'd been wounded and killed, all due to one kamikaze pilot. Reliving the event made him shiver and more and more he realized how lucky he was to be alive. One article he read said that the carrier was forced to leave the war due to her extensive damage and was on her way back to Bremerton for repairs.

The newspaper reported that Vice Admiral Mitscher praised the efforts of the damage control party by saying, "The attitude of the ship's company in combatting fire when under fire is indicative of the high order of efficiency that is rapidly winning the war."

In a conversation with his physical therapist one afternoon, Lou held up a newspaper. "I read an article in here that says the *Enterprise* changed the course of the war and was the most decorated ship of the Second World War." Lou smiled. "And to think I got to serve on her!"

Initially, Lou had tried to write letters home using his left hand, but that only produced a page of scribbles that not even he could decipher, so he asked a nurse if she'd mind writing what he dictated. She was happy to help him and together they kept his family apprised of his condition. With more physical therapy, he was finally able to write letters by himself using his right hand.

He looked forward to mail call every day now that mail was getting through to him on a more regular basis. One day alone he received four letters. His mom wrote that the members of the First Baptist Church were praying for him and all the other young men in the service. She continued, "We painted your room and added new curtains; we even got you a matching chenille bedspread that's going to make your room look inviting and ready for you. I don't know about your room, but I'm sure ready for you to come home, my dear sweet son. Do what the doctors say so you'll get well and come back to us quickly."

His dad wrote that with the war over in Germany, business was starting to pick up again. "Cadillac is making cars again and that's good news for us, especially now that the Depression has ended. People have money and we have the cars they want. I need you here, son, so get better soon."

One particular letter that brought a smile to Lou was from Anna. She was ecstatic that Ned was home.

The second half of the letter was written by Emma, overjoyed to have Joe home, and both men in one piece. Both girls wrote they were planning weddings, but were waiting for Lou to get home. "So get better and get your butt home!" added Emma. "We want to get married!" Lou laughed, picturing his sisters and the way they loved to tease him. Oh, how he missed them!

The fourth envelope had familiar lettering. He quickly tore it open to read what Gus had written. "Hi, there. You doing good, ya? Your parents tell me you got a Purple Heart. That's m'boy.

"It'll be good to have you home again. Don't know if you heard, but my boys are home now." Lou let out the breath he hadn't realized he'd been holding.

"Gus Jr.'s okay, just needs time to adjust to normalcy. His unit was in Germany liberating prisoners from the Buchenwald camp. Seems the men were nothing but skin and bones by the time the allies got to 'em. He don't like ta talk about it, but I can tell the sight affected him; he suffers from some terrible nightmares.

My boy Karl was in an Italian hospital for a while recuperating from a head wound. Seems a mortar shell exploded next to him while his unit was chasing Germans into the mountains somewhere near Florence. He has a ugly scar, but his eyes are okay. So now this long dark time is over and they're both home. Soon you'll be home, too, Chief, and I'm looking forward to it, ya?"

Lou smiled, remembering the Halloween many long years ago when Gus gave him that nickname.

231

Chapter Fifty-Nine

A nurse stopped in to Lou's room to tell him he had a visitor. Lou was sitting in a chair, raising and lowering a weight to strengthen his arm, but when she stepped aside, he stood and ran over to greet his friend, Danny. They embraced until tears streamed down both faces. They stood back, looked at each other, and embraced again.

Lou finally found his voice. "I can't believe it's you! I was afraid I'd never see you again. What're ya doing here?"

Danny wiped his eyes. "Buddy, I can't tell ya what a sight for sore eyes you are. I thought for a while you were a goner. You really put a scare in ta me." Danny looked his friend up and down. "Ya look pretty normal, you feeling okay?"

"Yeah. As soon as my arm's strong enough, I'll be going home."

"How's your head? It looked pretty brutal after the . . . incident."

"You saw that, huh? I'm just glad I got you out of the way in time. I didn't think, I just ran and shoved ya. Hope I didn't hurt ya."

"Yeah, about that. Thanks, Dyson. It's the bravest thing anyone's ever done for me."

Lou reached in the drawer and pulled out the Purple Heart. "I didn't do it for you, buddy, I did it so I could get this sweet little lady."

Danny poked him in the left arm. "Yeah. Right. Tell it to someone who believes ya." He reached his hand out. "Can I hold it?"

Lou placed the medal in Danny's hand and watched him turn it over and over.

"Wow! My hero."

"Sure. If I'd thought about it even for a split second, I might not a saved your sorry butt; I would've saved myself instead."

Side by side, the two friends walked out into the Oahu sunshine and sauntered along stone paths lined with tropical flowers.

Lou got serious. "Is the *Enterprise* repaired yet? Are you back on it?"

Danny shook his head. "She's still up in Washington. There was a lot of damage done to her. Don't know if she'll ever sail again, although they think she will. Me? I'm stationed here at Pearl while she gets fixed. I'd have been here sooner, but we had classes every day since we arrived a few weeks ago. Plus, it took a while to find out where they were keeping ya. They treating ya okay?"

"Let me see, I'm in Hawaii. It's not New Haven, but it's the next best thing. I can't wait to go home, though."

Near the end of July, a doctor examined Lou then set his clipboard down. "Well Dyson, looks like there's nothing more we can do for you."

"You mean—"

"I mean you oughtta get out of here and go home. Your medical discharge papers are ready and waiting for you. But first—"

"First?"

You need to put your uniform on tomorrow and go see the base commander. He's waiting to see you off. And make sure you wear your Purple Heart, too."

The next day, Lou packed his sea bag, checked to make sure he'd left nothing in the room, stepped outside and headed for the base. Part way there, he saw Danny running toward him.

"Whatcha doing here, Epstein? Think I've forgotten my way to the base?"

"You never know, it's been a while. Plus, you injured your head, so who knows what you remember. Let's go."

"Boy, you're in a big hurry to get rid of me. And I thought you were my friend."

"You won't get rid of me; I expect to avoid Buffalo winters by going south, all the way to New Haven once I get home. I hear your mom makes the best pies around." Danny ran his tongue over his lips. "I can taste 'em now."

They continued talking and as they approached the base, Lou noticed a crowd gathered on the lawn. Just being on a base again, gave Lou a sense of pride. He was torn between knowing he'd miss the Navy, yet wanting to go home.

An aide came over and motioned to Lou to follow him.

As Lou walked through the crowd, he noticed folding chairs arranged in rows. *Hmm,* he thought, *there must be something going on here later. Let me get my discharge papers and get out of their way.*

The aide motioned for Lou and Danny to sit in the front row. When everyone else had taken a seat, the base commander came out, faced the crowd, and approached the microphone.

The commander cleared his throat. "By order of the Secretary of the Navy, the Bronze Star Medal with valor is hereby awarded to Petty Officer Louis Dyson, No. 113996. This medal is awarded to Petty Officer Dyson for unwavering courage and commitment aboard the USS *Enterprise.* In the heat of battle and with no regard for his own life, he distinguished himself by saving the life of Fire Controlman Daniel Epstein, First Class. His bravery is in keeping with the finest traditions of military heroism and reflects credit upon himself and the United States Navy. Petty Officer Dyson, come forward and receive your Bronze Star."

Lou looked over at a grinning Danny who held his palms up in an "I didn't know" gesture while trying to feign innocence. Lou scowled at his friend, rose and walked up to the commander and offered a strong, crisp salute. The commander held up the medal, a bronze star attached to a red, white, and blue ribbon; in the center of the ribbon was a bronze V for Valor. On the reverse side of the star were the words: Heroic or Meritorious Achievement. As the medal was being

235

pinned on his uniform, Lou stood tall and erect, silently hoping his knees wouldn't buckle in front of everyone.

His brother's words calling him a hero echoed in his ears. Lou smiled. *I'm not a screw up after all.*

Epilogue

On a hot, muggy, August afternoon, a taxi pulled up to Fuller Street in New Haven. Lou, in full uniform, exited the cab and for a moment stood on the sidewalk staring at his home while memories flooded over him. Then he stepped inside and found banners, food, people, all cheering his homecoming. Even Hope was chirping a happy tune at his return.

He was expecting to be glad handed and welcomed back into the fold. What he wasn't prepared for were the emotions that engulfed him the moment his parents and sisters hugged him. Unapologetically, he let the tears stream down his face, only wiping them away when he looked around the room and saw Ned, Joe, Gus Jr. and Karl waiting to greet him.

The boys then stood aside to let Gus through. A wide smile on his face, Gus slowly shuffled toward him, raised his arm and smartly saluted him. Lou returned the salute then quickly stepped forward to give his lifelong friend and mentor a warm embrace.

A few days later, on August 9, a shout was heard across the country as word came over the radio that the war was over and America and her allies had won. People were excited at the thought of getting back to living normal lives, lives that didn't include being uprooted and perhaps killed or maimed. But if he had to do it again, Lou knew he would re-enlist in a heartbeat. The same sentiment was shared by Ned, Joe, Gus Jr. and Karl.

In September, the twins held a double wedding at the elaborately-decorated First Baptist Church. Mike proudly escorted Anna down the aisle while Lou escorted Emma amid all the guests and flowers. Laura sat in the front pew with a box of tissues that was quickly emptying.

Lou went back to work at the dealership, repairing both cars and motorcycles. Eventually, with the help of his G.I. Bill, he opened his own shop, Lou's Cycles, selling new and used motorcycles.

In the meantime, Lou rekindled his romance with Karen and, after a two-year courtship, popped the question. Danny came down from Buffalo to serve as Lou's best man while the twins served jointly as Karen's matrons of honor. After the wedding, Lou and Karen honeymooned in Maui where the first of their three little girls were conceived.

Twenty years later, Gary Haywood (*Finding Gary*) became one of Lou's best employees. Gary's close friend and motorcycle companion, Mark Fortier (*Leaving Mark)* had a daughter, Shelly, who bought an old house with her husband and remodeled it, finding clues to its past owners (*Willard Manor*).

About the author:

Linda Loegel is a born New Englander who now lives in Garner,
North Carolina. When she's not with friends at a weekly read and
critique group, she enjoys sitting on her back-porch swing
watching the birds and deer, a cup of coffee in hand. She finds joy
in reading, writing, traveling, eating dark chocolate, and being with
her three children, three grandchildren and four great
grandchildren.

She has authored eight books, including four novels.
Read her blog at www.lindaloegel.blogspot.com.

She is also on Facebook and Twitter.
You may contact her at lindaloegel@gmail.com

Books by Linda Loegel

Novels

Willard Manor

Leaving Mark

Finding Gary

Saving Lou

These books are all related to each other and help to fictionally populate the City of New Haven, CT in their particular historical context.

Other Books

The Devil Wore Plaid (marriage to an alcoholic hemophiliac)

Bumps Along the Way (a ten-thousand-mile cross country trip by car with two cranky seniors)

If you Don't Like Worms, Keep Your Mouth Shut (a story of growing up in a small town in Vermont in the 1940's)

Stop Procrastinating – Get Published! (a writer's guide to getting published)

Open Your Eyes to God's Beauty (a collection of four generations of poems)

Made in the USA
Columbia, SC
05 September 2017